KAY HOOPER

~

Rebel Waltz

BANTAM BOOKS

REBEL WALTZ
A Bantam Book

PUBLISHING HISTORY
Bantam Loveswept mass market edition published February 1986
Bantam mass market edition / April 2009

Published by Bantam Dell
A Division of Random House, Inc.
New York, New York

This is a work of fiction. Names, characters, places, and incidents
either are the product of the author's imagination or are used
fictitiously. Any resemblance to actual persons, living or dead,
events, or locales is entirely coincidental.

All rights reserved
Copyright © 1986 by Kay Hooper
Cover design by Yook Louie
Cover images © David Davis and John Wollwerth/Shutterstock

If you purchased this book without a cover, you should be aware
that this book is stolen property. It was reported as "unsold and
destroyed" to the publisher, and neither the author nor the publisher has received any payment for this "stripped book."

Bantam Books and the rooster colophon are registered trademarks
of Random House, Inc.

ISBN 978-0-553-59056-2

Printed in the United States of America
Published simultaneously in Canada

www.bantamdell.com

OPM 10 9 8 7 6 5 4 3 2 1

For Dee—
Who told me what to do with the toga

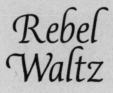

Rebel
Waltz

PRAISE FOR THE NOVELS OF

Kay Hooper

BLOOD DREAMS

"You won't want to turn the lights out after reading this book!" —*Romantic Times*

"A good read for fans of other serial-killer books and the TV show *Criminal Minds*." —*Booklist*

SLEEPING WITH FEAR

"An entertaining book for any reader."
—*Winston-Salem Journal*

"Hooper keeps the suspense dialed up....Readers will be mesmerized by a plot that moves quickly to a chilling conclusion." —*Publishers Weekly*

CHILL OF FEAR

"Hooper's latest may offer her fans a few shivers on a hot beach." —*Publishers Weekly*

"Kay Hooper has conjured a fine thriller with appealing young ghosts and a suitably evil presence to provide a welcome chill on a hot summer's day."
—*Orlando Sentinel*

"The author draws the reader into the story line and, once there, they can't leave because they want to see what happens next in this thrill-a-minute, chilling, fantastic reading experience." —*Midwest Book Review*

HUNTING FEAR

"A well-told scary story." —*Toronto Sun*

"Hooper's unerring story sense and ability to keep the pages flying can't be denied."
—*Ellery Queen Mystery Magazine*

"Hooper has created another original—*Hunting Fear* sets an intense pace....Work your way through the terror to the triumph...and you'll be looking for more Hooper tales to add to your bookshelf."
—*Wichita Falls (TX) Times Record News*

"It's vintage Hooper—a suspenseful page-turner."
—*Brazosport Facts*

"Expect plenty of twists and surprises as Kay Hooper gets her series off to a crackerjack start!"
—*Aptos Times*

SENSE OF EVIL

"A well-written, entertaining police procedural... loaded with suspense." —*Midwest Book Review*

"Filled with page-turning suspense."
—*Sunday Oklahoman*

"*Sense of Evil* will knock your socks off."
—*Rendezvous*

"A master storyteller." —Tami Hoag

STEALING SHADOWS

"A fast-paced, suspenseful plot . . . The story's complicated and intriguing twists and turns keep the reader
guessing until the chilling end." —*Publishers Weekly*

"This definitely puts Ms. Hooper in a league with
Tami Hoag and Iris Johansen and Sandra Brown.
Gold 5-star rating." —*Heartland Critiques*

HAUNTING RACHEL

"A stirring and evocative thriller."
—*Palo Alto Daily News*

"The pace flies, the suspense never lets up. It's great
reading." —*Baton Rouge Advocate*

"An intriguing book with plenty of strange twists
that will please the reader." —*Rocky Mountain News*

"It passed the 'stay up late to finish it in one night'
test." —*Denver Post*

FINDING LAURA

"You always know you are in for an outstanding read
when you pick up a Kay Hooper novel, but in
Finding Laura, she has created something really special! Simply superb!" —*Romantic Times*

"Hooper keeps the intrigue pleasurably complicated,
with gothic touches of suspense and a satisfying reso-
lution." —*Publishers Weekly*

"A first-class reading experience."
—*Affaire de Coeur*

AFTER CAROLINE

"Harrowing good fun. Readers will shiver and shudder." —*Publishers Weekly*

"Kay Hooper has crafted another solid story to keep readers enthralled until the last page is turned."
                                        —*Booklist*

"Kay Hooper comes through with thrills, chills, and plenty of romance, this time with an energetic murder mystery with a clever twist. The suspense is sustained admirably right up to the very end."
                                        —*Kirkus Reviews*

BANTAM BOOKS BY KAY HOOPER

The Bishop Trilogies
Stealing Shadows
Hiding in the Shadows
Out of the Shadows

Touching Evil
Whisper of Evil
Sense of Evil

Hunting Fear
Chill of Fear
Sleeping with Fear

Blood Dreams
Blood Sins

The Quinn Novels
Once a Thief
Always a Thief

Romantic Suspense
Amanda
After Caroline
Finding Laura
Haunting Rachel

Classic Fantasy and Romance
On Wings of Magic
The Wizard of Seattle
My Guardian Angel *(anthology)*
Yours to Keep *(anthology)*
Golden Threads
Something Different
Pepper's Way
C.J.'s Fate
The Haunting of Josie
Illegal Possession
If There Be Dragons

ONE

SPANISH MOSS HUNG from the towering trees, draping branches, shadowing the drive in coolness. It should have looked gloomy, but didn't, somehow. Sunlight filtered through the leaves and moss to create a mosaic on the hard-packed ground.

Rory stood leaning against the opened car door, gazing around and noting that Nature had been allowed to encroach on what had once, probably, been stunningly beautiful land. The woods were now thickly grown with brambles and nearly impassable; the distant pasture, although obviously still cultivated for hay, was surrounded by a once-white three-rail fence that looked more imagined than real; a gazebo nearly invisible beneath years of ivy strove valiantly to remain standing; and the driveway was packed dirt with not a trace of gravel or pavement, but many a deep rut.

His cool gray eyes measuring, Rory calculated what it would take to restore the land. A riding path through the woods, he mused, and a footpath and benches for guests in need of shaded solitude. The old gazebo torn down and another constructed. The stables weren't visible, but probably they, too, would need a major overhaul.

He thought of the other plantations he'd purchased and converted into resort-type hotels, then looked steadily up the tree-lined drive to the house. Outwardly, it was in better shape than most of the few remaining privately owned plantations. It possessed wide, shallow steps, a veranda extending along two sides, solid white

Doric columns, and the landscaping near the building *had* been kept up. Red brick mellowed by time was decorated here and there by climbing ivy. The shutters appeared to be in good repair and there were no broken windows in sight.

Although heaven only knew what rotten floorboards and moldy draperies awaited him inside... Jasmine Hall's noble owner had never allowed cameras inside the place, so Rory hadn't the faintest idea what he'd find.

Sighing, he got back into the car and continued up the drive. He'd stay two weeks, as invited, he decided, to look the place over and find out if old Jake Clairmont was really serious this time about selling Jasmine Hall.

Twice before, the crusty old man had spread the word, only to back out gleefully when Rory and others had expressed interest in buying. The second time had been in Charleston, nearly a year before. The third time, six weeks ago, no one but Rory had taken the bait. And he was still vaguely surprised and slightly suspicious that he had been promptly invited out to visit the estate.

He frowned as he parked the car in the graveled area near the house and got out, wondering if Clairmont had been foxy enough to have weeded out less interested parties by offering to sell the first two times and then retracting his offer.

It put Rory on guard, his keen business sense wary of an attempt to drive up the price. Although, of course, the place *was* priceless.

Pushing the thought aside, he went up the broad, shallow steps and made use of the shining brass knocker. He had to use it three times, the third time with considerable force, before the heavy solid-oak door finally swung open. And in that moment Rory experienced the somewhat bewildering shock of a man whose entire attention was quite forcibly ripped from all thoughts of business.

She was an antebellum Southern belle, complete from the raven hair dressed in ringlets to the silk slippers peeping from the hem of her hoop skirt. The gown was emerald silk, off the shoulders and breathtakingly low-cut, and the faint rustle of each movement announced the presence of at least a dozen petticoats. Her face was heart-shaped and delicate, each feature finely drawn by an appreciative artist. She seemed young, perhaps in her early twenties, although the costume might have been deceptive.

And Rory thought dizzily that Scarlett O'Hara had a rival here in green eyes and an impossibly tiny waist.

"Whatever you're selling, we don't want any."

If her voice was soft and drawling, her tone at least was thoroughly modern and more than a little impatient. And there was faint surprise in her eyes as she stared up at him, a tiny frown of puzzlement on her forehead.

Rory pulled himself together with determination, leaving his questions for later. "My name's Stewart—Rory Stewart. Mr. Clairmont is expecting me."

"Oh." Sea-green eyes looked him up and

down thoughtfully—and with faint hostility?—before focusing on his face. "You're early; we weren't expecting you until tomorrow," she said abruptly.

Rory ignored the rudeness. "I finished my business in Charleston this morning and decided to get an early start. Unless that's inconvenient, Miss—?"

"Clairmont. Banner Clairmont. Jake's my grandfather."

Uncomfortably aware of the measuring green eyes holding that slight animosity, Rory reminded himself sternly that Scarlett O'Hara had been a lady only skin deep...and sometimes not even that. "If it's inconvenient—?" he repeated steadily.

"No. No, I suppose not." She stepped back, gown rustling, and allowed him into the foyer. "Come in."

Rory's second shock came upon entering the house. He was experienced in detecting attempts to camouflage decaying old mansions with paint and paper in order to have them fetch a higher price, and knew full well that most Southern families never sold out until they simply could not afford the upkeep of their mansions. He had assumed Jake Clairmont to be in that majority, after seeing the condition of the property surrounding the house.

But Jasmine Hall was fully restored and absolutely beautiful.

He stood in silence, staring about him, his innate love of these historic old homes nearly overpowering him as he saw the foyer as it was meant to be and probably had been a century before.

The wide twin staircases flanking either side of the vast foyer, polished wood gleaming and thick carpet deeply red and spotless. The sparkling chandelier. The antique tables holding priceless vases and figurines. The Old Masters hanging on the walls. The marble floor dotted here and there with intricately woven rugs.

A myriad of thoughts crowded Rory's mind. The old man was toying with him; he couldn't mean to sell this treasure. If he could afford to maintain it in this prime condition...It would cost the earth if Clairmont *were* serious. But... dear Lord, wouldn't he love to own this! He'd mortgage practically everything he possessed to have this house. And no resort hotel *here*. No, this was a home meant to hold a family. But there was no way he possibly could justify the expense; it was impractical and impossible and...and damn Clairmont for the tormenting old devil he was.

Only then did Rory snap out of his trance and realize that the "old devil's" granddaughter had been watching him steadily. He fought to hide what must have been hunger in his eyes, turning to her and waiting politely for her to lead the way. He was faintly surprised to observe that her animosity had vanished, to be replaced by a speculative curiosity, but she gave him no opportunity to probe it.

"This way," she said, gesturing for him to follow as she headed across the foyer to a set of huge, beautifully carved double doors. She flung one of them open, rustling into a room revealed to be a library as beautifully restored as the foyer and announcing with a hint of mockery in her soft voice. "You have a visitor, Jake."

Rising from a leather wing chair by the fireplace, Jake Clairmont set aside the book he'd apparently been reading and immediately came forward with hand outstretched to greet Rory. He was a benign old man in appearance, tall and slender, with a full head of silver hair and the slightly leathery skin of a man who'd spent most of his life outdoors. His lean body was hard and still powerful though he was in his sixties, and he moved with certainty and grace. The mild serenity of his expression was belied by the acuteness of his vivid green eyes.

Quite suddenly, Rory remembered overhearing from the lips of one of Clairmont's closest friends that Jake was half hawk and half shark, and that the only living soul capable of making him bow to another's wishes was the granddaughter he adored.

"Rory. Glad you could make it, my boy. Welcome."

The "my boy," Rory reflected musingly, would have been patronizing from anyone else's lips; from Clairmont it sounded entirely natural and amiable. Suspicious, Rory wondered what the old shark was up to. "Thank you, Jake," he responded mildly. "It's good to see you again."

"You've met Banner, I see." Half statement, half question.

Glancing toward the fireplace, where Banner stood with a disquieting look of amusement on her lovely face, Rory nodded. "I've had that pleasure," he confirmed, and wondered why he always felt somewhat like a Regency gent whenever he was around Jake; they had met several times in Charleston, and on each occasion he'd felt an alarming attack of careful manners sweeping over him. Perhaps it was the Old World quality in Jake's own behavior.

The damned old rogue could rob you blind and leave you with a smile, he thought with an inner laugh.

"Good, good." Jake seemed inordinately pleased. "She can give you a quick tour of the house while I have someone bring in your bags. I'm sure you'll want to wander around by yourself tomorrow, but Banner can tell you quite a bit about our history."

Before Rory could respond, Banner did.

"Jake, have you forgotten the party? I *do* have a few things to take care of before our guests arrive."

Her grandfather waved the remark away. "Plenty of time for that. Besides, you look so beautiful nobody's going to notice anything else."

While Rory watched in silence, two pairs of green eyes locked in a silent struggle that was almost palpable. Both combatants smiled easily and gazed steadily, and Rory didn't dare wager to himself who would win. He just waited.

Finally, Banner sighed and turned away to head for the door. "This way, Mr. Stewart," she said wryly.

Rory only just stopped himself from bowing to the smiling Jake before following the girl from the room.

Once out in the foyer, she began speaking in a cool, faintly insolent tone that grated and was, Rory thought, quite deliberate. And she sounded for all the world like a bored tour guide.

"The main house was restored ten years ago; until that time it had been kept up structurally but the interior had been neglected. Now, each room has been painstakingly restored; all furnishings are period pieces and all materials authentic. There are thirty rooms, including library, study, a formal dining room, ballroom, several sitting rooms and dens, and bedrooms. Only the bathrooms are not authentic, and those have been designed to blend in as much as possible. Where d'you want to start, Mr. Stewart?"

He gazed down at her bland, inquiring face, and said pleasantly, "If you'll just direct me to my room, I'll leave you to get ready for your party. We can skip the tour for now."

"My grandfather requested it," she reminded him coolly.

"Sounded more like an order to me."

She shrugged slightly, whether in agreement

or disagreement or mere acknowledgment of his comment he couldn't tell.

Ignoring his suggestion that the tour could wait, Banner said briskly, "We'll start with the ballroom." And she led the way.

For the first time in his memory, Rory paid scant attention to the tour and quite a bit to the guide. She seemed intent on alienating him— or at the very least angering him. Every word seemed calculated in tone to rouse defensiveness and aggression. She was cold, rude, patronizing, and impatient.

Rory was not a man to stand for that kind of thing, but he stood it from Banner Clairmont. He met coldness with amiability, rudeness with impeccable manners, condescension with blandness. He ignored her impatience, asked few questions, and came to the conclusion that his first impression had been the correct one.

Banner was not innately rude, cold, patronizing, or even unfriendly. She was deliberately trying to provoke him. He hadn't a shadow of an idea why she wanted to, unless it was because he was interested in buying Jasmine Hall and she didn't want it sold. He let that thought rest in the back of his mind for later study, while the tour continued.

There was quite a bit of activity throughout the house in preparation for the party. Servants in antebellum dress scurried about carrying flowers and linens and food, getting in one another's way and being stridently polite about it.

And Rory was more than a little curious. "Jake didn't mention a party," he said carefully as Banner was conducting him through the bedroom wing of the huge house. "I would certainly have waited until tomorrow to come if I'd known."

Banner sent him an inscrutable look. "You'll find a costume on your bed," she said calmly.

"What? But—"

"Jake's always prepared," she added cryptically.

"I don't want to intrude," Rory ventured.

She ignored that. "There'll be a couple of hundred guests at the party," she said, "and about fifty staying the night. Tomorrow morning we'll have a hunt; you'll find a riding costume in your closet. You do ride?" she added on a questioning note.

"As it happens, I do," he said, stung for the first time.

She smiled an odd little smile. "I'll be sure to pick out a good hunter for you."

Rory looked at her suspiciously.

Halting before an open door, Banner gestured inside. "This is your room. Your bags have been unpacked. If you need anything, just pull the bell rope. The party is scheduled to start in two hours; we're serving a light supper downstairs in the little dining room in thirty minutes. If you decide to skip that, there'll be food served during the party."

Half-expecting her to add, "Any questions?" Rory took a deep breath and struggled to hang on to his manners. And lost. "You don't like me very much, do you?" he said abruptly.

"I just met you," she answered coolly.

"If you treat everyone this way on first meeting them," he noted, "you must make a lot of enemies."

"Only my share," she said sweetly.

Rory strove with himself. "I don't enjoy being treated like a pariah, Miss Clairmont," he said in the most even tone he could manage.

Her smile was limpid. "Why, Mr. Stewart— we never invite pariahs to our parties."

"I wasn't invited," he snapped.

"Do tell." She was still smiling.

Rory glanced around, wondering with that unfamiliar savagery if there would be witnesses to imminent homicide. He restrained his impulses when he saw several couples at the end of the hallway descending the stairs from the third floor and apparently on their way to the ballroom. He noted absently that the men seemed to be wearing Civil War uniforms—Rebel Gray, of course.

"There go some of your guests down the

stairs. You'd better see to them," he muttered. "They seem to be early."

Banner followed his gaze, and Rory felt more than saw her start slightly, as if in surprise. When she looked back up at him, there was an arrested, almost panicky expression in her green eyes. "Yes," she said softly. "Yes, I'd better do that."

That look in her eyes bothered him. "Banner—" he began, hardly aware of using her first name.

She interrupted him, her voice still soft. "If you have any trouble with your costume, Jake's valet will help you. Just pull the bell rope. I'll see you downstairs." She hurried down the hall, silk gown rustling quietly.

Rory gazed after her for a long moment, then shrugged almost irritably and went into his bedroom, wondering vaguely why the very masculine bedroom smelled of jasmine.

TWO

BANNER CLOSED THE library doors by leaning back against them, looking across the room at her grandfather, who was now in costume and looked every inch the Southern plantation owner.

He smiled at her with just a trace of wicked mischief. "How'd the tour go?" he inquired.

"Oh, just dandy." Banner's cheerful voice was a far cry from the cold tone of the tour. "I was horribly rude to your Mr. Stewart and he took it like a gent." She laughed suddenly. "Until a couple of minutes ago, that is."

"Did he flay you?" Jake Clairmont asked interestedly.

"He wanted to murder me! However, since he's a guest in your house...At least, that's the impression I got." Banner hesitated, then said in a determinedly toneless voice, "He...saw the soldiers and their brides, Grandfather."

Jake's gaze sharpened, the same arrested expression Rory had seen in Banner's eyes in his now. "Did he?" the old man murmured thoughtfully. "Did he, now? That's interesting."

"He thought they were our guests."

"You didn't tell him...?"

"No, of course not." In a voice suddenly passionate with feeling, Banner exclaimed, "Jake, you can't sell to him! This place is in your blood—in *mine*. It'd kill us both to leave."

Jake looked at her for a moment, then shrugged. "He came out here in good faith, you know that. I offered to sell, he wants to buy. If his price is right—"

"He'll be master of Jasmine Hall," she finished bitterly.

Flatly, Jake said, "Restoring the place took a huge chunk out of our capital, Banner, and it'll take more than we've got left to turn the Hall into a paying plantation." Deliberately, brutally, he added, "D'you want to see it decay like the others in this area?"

"No," she whispered.

"Then we have two choices. We can turn the place over to a historical society or we can sell to someone like Rory Stewart, who's interested in keeping it relatively intact."

Banner squared her shoulders, the reason of his words sinking in against her will. She smiled at him, hiding heartbreak and showing her Clairmont blood and her love for the old man in her affectionate words. "You old bastard."

Jake grinned at her. "I promised I wouldn't sell the place without your approval, lass, and I meant it. We'll take a long, hard look at Stewart before we decide. We'll make sure we leave the Hall in good hands. Agreed?"

"Agreed, Grandfather."

"All right, then." He lifted a quizzical brow at her. "And none of your tricks, Banner."

"I don't play tricks," she said indignantly.

Jake Clairmont smiled faintly. "When you were ten," he reminded her, "you very innocently proclaimed that the Hall was haunted, because you wanted to discourage potential buyers."

"That was seventeen years ago," she pointed out virtuously. "I didn't know that you weren't serious about selling and I was *not* playing tricks."

"Well, be nice to Stewart. No more rudeness, all right?"

Banner tossed her head and turned to open the door. "Of course I'll be nice," she said loftily over her shoulder. "I've already short-sheeted his bed, disconnected the hot water in his bathroom, and put thorns in the seat of his riding breeches—how much nicer could I be?"

She closed the door behind her, hearing her grandfather laugh. She listened to the growing clamor of the party preparations and, after a moment of indecision and a guilty glance at the clock near the stairs, hurried out of the house through the French doors in the front parlor. She crossed the veranda and went down the steps and through the rose garden, holding up her skirts and following a path that led into the woods.

She wound up at a little cottage built in a clearing less than a hundred yards from the main house. According to the Hall books, the cottage had been built before the Civil War, but Banner had never been able to find out just why it existed. As a child, she'd woven stories of lovers' trysts and family disapproval, and saw no reason now to reconsider the stories. They suited both her romantic nature and the cosy architecture of the cottage.

In good repair, the little house was nestled among the trees, peeping like a shy maiden from behind her fan. It had been Banner's "pretend" house as a child, and as she'd grown she had made it her sanctuary. It contained a single bedroom—the bed kept ready in case she chose to sleep there—and one large open area that Banner had made into a workroom. The bathroom had been built a few years ago and was the only modern part of the structure.

Banner stood on tiptoe to find the key resting above the doorjamb, then unlocked the door, replaced the key, and went inside. She left the door open out of habit, secure in the knowledge that no one ever disturbed her here.

In the main room of the cottage, she quickly removed the ringlet-dressed wig she wore and hung it rather comically over a bust of her grandfather, which had been one of her few early attempts to sculpt. She ran her fingers through her own short raven curls, massaging her scalp absently as she stared at the half-finished painting on the easel in the center of the room. She longed to sit down and frown at her work in earnest, but lacked the time and was reluctant to crush the silk gown.

So she just stood, rubbing a scalp that was itching from its confinement by the wig, and glared at her portrait. Why, she wondered, did it look so awfully damned much like Rory Stewart? That was what had brought her out here to stare even though she'd little time for it. She'd started on the thing days ago, and had intended merely to portray a Southern gentleman, to paint him entirely from her own mind.

Dammit, it looked like Rory Stewart!

Thick, sun-lightened blond hair—and she didn't even *like* blond men. Level gray eyes. A lean, strong face with compelling bone structure. Crooked smile. Proud tilt to his head. Only the attire was different; this man was dressed in the well-cut, long-tailed coat and ruffled shirt of the Southern beau out to break hearts—

"That wig's a crime."

Banner turned so quickly that she nearly lost her balance, staring toward the door and thinking, *Damn—it really is him.*

Rory had changed into the costume provided by Clairmont, and not only did it fit him perfectly, it also suited him perfectly. From the smooth crown of his thick blond hair to the mirror reflection of his black boots, he was the personification of a Southern gentleman.

"What?" she managed to ask, then realized that she was still massaging her head. Quickly, she let her hands drop.

"I said that wig's a crime," he repeated patiently, studying the thick curls that lent her small head a deceptively fragile look.

Banner considered resurrecting her hostility, but abandoned the notion. There would be time for animosity, she decided, *after* he bought Jasmine Hall—*if* he bought it. She therefore obviously startled him with a sunny smile. "The wig itches," she confided solemnly.

Rory blinked, torn between the instant pleasure of her smile and an uneasy suspicion about her change in attitude. "I hope you don't mind," he said rather abruptly. "I saw you from my window and wondered where you were going." He glanced around, then added carefully, "I don't want to intrude."

She wondered briefly at his odd tone, then dismissed it. "This is where I work," she explained.

"Do you paint professionally?" he asked, looking at all the canvases propped against the walls.

"It's more of a hobby, really. I'm not good enough to be a pro."

Rory stared at her for an incredulous moment, then went over to one particularly thick stack of canvases, went down on one knee, and began looking through them. When he finally rose to his feet, he turned to stare at her again. He realized in some surprise that she honestly had no idea of just how good she was.

"Has Jake seen these?" he asked.

Banner shrugged. "I haven't shown him anything but sketches in a long time. Why?"

"Because they're brilliant," Rory said flatly.

She felt a flush rising in her cheeks. "I'm just a hobbyist," she told him uncomfortably.

He decided to drop the subject—for the moment. He moved around the easel until he could see the painting she'd been studying when he came in, startled to find himself gazing on what could have been a portrait of himself. "Hello. What in the world—?"

"Odd, isn't it?" she said. "I can't understand it. I was just imagining a Southern gent, and that's what I ended up with."

"Oh? I thought perhaps your friend—?"

She blinked at him. "What friend? What're you talking about?"

Rory looked at her, puzzled. "The man who walked across the rose garden with you. He was dressed like this"—he gestured at the painting—"and was blond. Where is he, by the way?"

Banner very carefully backed up a step and half-sat on a tall stool, unmindful, now, of her gown. She reflected in a queerly detached manner that Rory's earlier comment about "intruding" now made sense; he'd been wary of walking in on a lovers' tryst. "Oh...I'm alone, Mr. Stewart," she murmured.

"Rory," he corrected automatically, trying to pin down her expression and deciding at last that it was a curious blend of laughter and bemusement. "Your friend's gone, then?"

"Mmmm," she offered noncommittally.

Conscious of the odd feeling that he was missing something, Rory gazed at her and tried again. "It's strange that your painting looks so much like me, Miss Clairmont. Of course, there are differences."

"Are there? We never see ourselves as others see us, do we?" she commented cryptically, then went on, "Might as well make it Banner, all right? And I really think we should be going back to the house, Mr.—um—Rory."

"Certainly," he agreed, watching as she removed the wig from a wickedly accurate bust of her grandfather and expertly pulled it on over her own short curls. He wanted to ask what had become of her friend—in fact, he was surprised at just how much he wanted to question her about the man—but held his peace. Since he'd entered the cottage, she'd been not only polite, but actually friendly, and he didn't want to put her back up inadvertently.

Banner led the way out of the little house, locking the door behind them but making no attempt to disguise from Stewart where the key was kept. They went through the rose garden and into the house through the French doors, finding that the party chaos had intensified alarmingly.

Wincing as the sound of something fragile crashing smote their ears, Banner gestured for Stewart to follow her. "We'll go into the little dining room; Jake's probably waiting for us."

Jake was, in fact, waiting for them in the dining room that was intended for and used when only a few people were to be served meals. It was small and cosy, the antique table, chairs, and sideboard scaled exactly for a family group. And Banner's grandfather was so patently delighted to see them come into the room together—and obviously on friendly terms—that her good humor very nearly deserted her.

"I was showing Rory the garden," she said without thinking, then felt a flush creep up her face.

However, Jake Clairmont could hardly have managed to look more pleased whatever she'd said; he merely grinned and asked Rory what he thought of the estate roses.

That topic and Jasmine Hall in general lasted them throughout the light meal. Banner said nothing; she watched Jake rather broodingly, her eyes flicking toward Rory occasionally and holding a speculative expression.

And it wasn't until they had risen from the table and headed back toward the foyer and the sounds of guests arriving that Rory abruptly realized why Jake Clairmont had been so pleased and why Banner had fallen so unaccountably silent. His first thought as understanding dawned was, That old shark! His second thought—and a ruefully annoyed one at that—was, This is going to complicate things hellishly. This is *definitely* going to complicate things. He was made absolutely certain of just how complicated "things" already were when he heard Banner take a moment to hiss wrathfully into her grandfather's ear.

"What you're up to, Jake, you can just forget."

Jake didn't seem noticeably abashed, but

Rory was conscious of a strong desire to throttle the old man. Anyone but an idiot, he thought, could see that Banner was going to refuse to have anything further to do with him after her grandfather's intent had been made so painfully obvious.

The old devil was matchmaking, for God's sake!

Rory thought of several things in that moment. He thought that his own plans might now be equated with a salmon's struggle to swim upstream. He thought morosely about the unknown blond man in the rose garden. And he wondered whether it had been Fate's intention or Clairmont's to strew boulders in his path.

"Damn," he muttered to himself. "I haven't got a ghost of a chance."

Within an hour, the party was in full swing. Since nobody had bothered to explain anything to him, Rory'd had to discover for himself that this was a yearly affair at Jasmine Hall; the entire neighborhood and anybody else who could manage to wangle an invitation turned up in full antebellum dress to pay tribute to bygone years. Some came only for the party; others intended to spend the night to participate in the costumed hunt the next morning.

Since Rory and Jake moved in some of the same business circles he found there were quite a few people present whom he knew. But as the guests began pouring fast and thick into the house, he started to worry that Banner and her grandfather seemed blithely unconcerned about the likelihood of gate-crashers.

He finally managed to locate Banner in the crush of people and to draw her into an alcove in the ballroom. "I don't mean to pry," he announced firmly, "but have you and Jake thought much about gate-crashers, Banner?"

"Oh, there are always gate-crashers," she told him cheerfully.

Rory was abruptly conscious that hers was an impersonal cheerfulness, and spared a moment for a silent curse at Jake's heavy-handedness.

With an effort, he kept his voice as easy as hers. "Well, then, crass as it may sound, shouldn't someone keep an eye on the valuables?"

"Someone is," she assured him. "Several someones, in fact." She nodded toward the ballroom. "See the gent in maroon velvet? And the one in gray—and the one by the doors there—and—oh, and several others. They're private security guards."

"I see." Rory grinned slightly. "I should have known Jake wasn't all *that* trusting."

"Trusting?" Banner gazed up at him in astonishment. "*Jake?* Listen, my grandfather is a shark with a full set of teeth," she said roundly.

Laughing at the probably accurate but hardly filial summation, Rory quickly caught her hand when she would have turned away. "I seem to hear a waltz," he remarked musingly. "May I, Miss Clairmont?"

She blinked and then tried a laugh that didn't sound quite as gaily unconcerned as she'd intended. "Why not?"

Rory swept her out onto the floor among the

colorful array of laughing couples, proving himself to be an excellent dancer and also proving that he was perfectly capable of carrying on a conversation without having to count steps or mind his feet. His excellence depressed Banner for some reason she didn't try to fathom.

"Have you ever noticed that adults love an opportunity to dress up and pretend they belong to another age?" he was asking cheerfully.

"It's strange, isn't it?" she agreed. "And after spending so much time growing up, too." Banner, with some years of Jasmine Hall costume balls behind her, also had no need to count steps. However, she was ridiculously conscious of his hand at her waist and of the strength of his shoulder beneath her own hand. *Idiot*, she chided herself.

"I haven't seen your friend since the party began."

Banner started slightly, and as some response seemed called for, tried to dredge one up. "I—expect he's around here somewhere."

Rory looked pointedly at her left hand. "No ring," he observed.

She toyed briefly with the notion of using the blond man as a shield, then abandoned it. Just because her grandfather had an absurd idea about a romantic involvement between her and this very self-assured man dancing with her, it didn't mean that Rory shared it, she decided firmly. "He isn't—um—that kind of friend," she explained casually.

"I see." Rory nodded. "That's good."

In spite of herself, Banner had to bite her tongue to keep from taking the bait. But she managed. "You dance very well," she complimented hastily.

"Thank you. So do you. You're also dandy at changing the subject."

She was also very good at ignoring ungentlemanly teasing. Daring him with a frown to persist, she said briskly, "If there's anyone in particular you'd like to dance with or be introduced to, just let me know."

"When's the last dance of the evening?" he asked instantly.

"Midnight. By tradition a waltz."

"I'd definitely like to dance then."

"Oh? Well—"

"With you."

"I can't," she said apologetically, both glad and regretful that she had to refuse. "Another tradition—that's my dance with Jake."

Rory didn't seem noticeably disappointed. "Really? Well, my loss."

"Thanks," she muttered.

The musicians brought the dance to a re-sounding conclusion just then, and Rory, staying firmly in character as a Southern gent, bowed deeply and gracefully from the waist. "Thank you, ma'am," he said gravely.

"You're welcome," she said with something of a snap, and quickly, irritated with herself, went off to see to her guests.

Retiring to the sidelines to watch the next dance, Rory caught Jake Clairmont's ridiculously paternal eye on him. He returned the stare squarely for a moment, then purposefully crossed the room to speak to the older man.

The party had grown more cheerfully boisterous with every hour that had passed. Since the refreshments provided were lavishly democratic, more than one guest had succumbed and been escorted discreetly upstairs to a bed, either by a wife, husband, friend, or one of Clairmont's polite security guards.

Rory, amused and awed by the entire anachronous spectacle, wondered if anyone else appreciated this regression to another era in much more than dress. Some of the guests seemed enormously comfortable with their antebellum manners; there were several hot and rather tipsy disputes on whether or not the South really *should* secede, one lengthy discussion between two middle-aged men on Mr. Lincoln's merits, and one duel narrowly avoided when Banner stepped between the two combatants, saying cheerfully that she'd have no blood in the rose garden.

Not that there really would have been a duel. At least, Rory *hoped* there wouldn't have been a duel. For a dizzy moment, he wondered if he'd stepped back in time. The twentieth century, he realized in astonishment, began just outside those tremendous oak doors; inside this house, the Grand Old South reigned supreme—for this night, at least.

And it was fascinating to watch.

Rory had studied antebellum architecture and furnishings extensively, but his knowledge of the manners and morals of the day was culled entirely from fictional reading. He was therefore delighted and intrigued to see both displayed before him with an accuracy he didn't for a moment doubt.

No single young lady, he noticed—deducing "singleness" by the absence of rings—danced more than twice with any young man; older gentlemen gathered in groups near the refreshment table and talked brisk business; older ladies—

Matrons! he thought delightedly—sat along the walls talking and keeping wary eyes on daughters and on other ladies' sons. There was a great deal of lightly drawled flirtation and the batting of eyelashes over the edges of fans, and the dancing was decorous to the point of hilarity.

Banner, as the daughter of the house, moved among the guests, busily finding partners for wallflowers and keeping conversations going. Jake held court by the punch bowl.

Rory surprised a giggle from his hostess at one point, catching her in passing to ask incredulously, "Where did you *find* these people? Did you hire actors to put on a play, or what?"

"Aren't they wonderful? It's the same every year, and I just love it. The overnighters will be a bit sheepish in the morning, but once they're back in costume and on their horses they'll revert again."

"Tell me I'm in the twentieth century," Rory begged, half seriously.

Banner giggled again. "Wait until the party guests start to leave," she advised. "No carriages will pull up to the front door—only good old Detroit motorcars." Then she was off once more.

Rory didn't catch her after that until just before midnight, and then it was his determined intention to catch her. He pulled her firmly into the alcove he'd made use of before, saying to her questioning look, "I have to warn you."

"Warn me? What about?"

"Well, I know you're too much of a lady to make a scene," he explained, both astonished and amused to find himself reverting, just like everyone else, "but I think I should be a gentleman and not let you be—uh—caught off guard."

"By what?" she asked.

The musicians were winding up for another conclusion, and Rory said hurriedly, "By our dance."

Banner glanced at a nearby clock and said patiently, "I'm sorry, but I told you the last dance was Jake's."

"Not this time," Rory told her, a little guilty and a lot triumphant. "Tonight, the last dance is mine."

After staring up at him for a long moment, she said carefully, "Rory, you don't understand. It's a tradition. If you dance with me, everyone'll think that we—"

"Too late," he interrupted firmly as the musicians struck up the final waltz. Then he swept her out onto the floor.

Banner was given only a second to think, and that wasn't enough time. She saw her grandfather watching with a satisfied smile and a faintly sheepish light in his green eyes; she sent him the dirtiest look she could manage without losing her smile. She was very conscious of the speculative attention following them around the floor and wondered wryly if Rory had any idea at all of what he'd just proclaimed to the neighborhood—and to any gate-crasher who happened to be acquainted with Jasmine Hall tradition. After all, it *is* the twentieth century, she reminded herself sternly.

"Doesn't it bother you to be dancing alone, with everyone watching?" she asked him politely.

Rory laughed. "We do seem to be the center of attention," he commented. "But since the soldiers and their partners have come out of the woodwork to keep us company, we're not entirely alone. I wonder where they've been all evening," he added parenthetically.

Banner glanced around, hearing herself laugh a bit unsteadily and not at all surprised by it.

"Is something wrong?" he asked curiously, looking down at her.

"Hmmm? Oh. No, nothing's wrong." Banner got a grip on herself. "If you're interested, this ball is a tradition going all the way back to the Civil War," she offered.

He was interested. "Really?"

"Yes." Banner divided her attention between his gray eyes and the top of his ruffled shirt. "It was the last ball in this area before the War; actually, it was held the night before all the men marched off. And it was the last time all the families were together. During the War, of course, there weren't any balls. Jasmine Hall was the first to—um—resume the tradition; although I imagine the first ball after the War was more sad than gay."

Rory thought of the heartbreaking end to that tragic time and nodded. "Yes. So many men gone. So many widows dressed in black."

Banner stole a glance at his grave face. "I think perhaps I should tell you about another tradition begun that night," she said dryly.

"What is it?"

She could hear the musicians beginning to wind down, and timed her explanation perfectly. "Well, it just so happened that the son and daughter of the family got engaged that night— like so many young men and women. Anyway, the—uh—betrothed couples claimed the honor of the last dance. Ever since then, the last dance has been reserved for the master of the house and either his wife or daughter. Or, in my case, his granddaughter. And if a single daughter or son of the house dances with another gentleman or lady, it's only because they've become engaged. Until tonight," she added wryly as the music came to a close, "the tradition remained unbroken."

Stepping back from her startled partner, Banner curtsied deeply and gracefully. "Don't be surprised to receive hearty congratulations from the other guests," she advised him sweetly.

Rory watched her make her escape, having gotten a pretty good idea of the meaning behind both her words and the martial glint in her lovely green eyes. He turned his head slowly, scanning faces until he located Jake Clairmont. *Here's another fine mess you've gotten me into!* he sent silently to that old rascal. And another misunderstanding, he reflected wryly, to clear up. He decided to speak to Jake before either of them was much older.

Otherwise they'd neither of them get what both, apparently, very much wanted.

THREE

It was two a.m. The last of the home-going guests had stumbled or been poured into waiting cars, with the elected sober at the wheels. The overnighters had gradually, sometimes unsteadily, and certainly reluctantly gone up to their assigned rooms. Cleanup having been postponed until the next morning, the servants—Jasmine Hall's and those borrowed or hired for the occasion—had called it a night and gone off to bed. The musicians, paid and tipped, had packed up noisily and left.

And Banner, who had slipped away to remove her bulky costume as the last guests were dispersing, had returned to the library, where she knew her grandfather would be enjoying a few solitary moments before going to bed. She was going to have it out with him.

She was barefooted, and dressed for bed in a fashionably overlarge sleep shirt that fell off one shoulder and hung to her knees, making her look even more petite than she was. And the martial light Rory had seen in her eyes had achieved the dubious distinction of looking very like the fires of hell.

"You *planned* it. I know you, Jake; you planned the whole damned thing."

"How could I have done that?" her injured grandsire wondered mildly from the depths of his comfortable chair. "Rory asked me if he could take my place in the dance. What was I supposed to say?"

"No," she snapped. "And you could have

explained to him about the tradition. But did you? Of course not. You made fools out of both of us!"

"Did I?" He smiled slightly, watching her. "How?"

"The whole neighborhood thinks we're engaged!" Banner yelped. "And, yes, I denied it. Who believed me? Nobody, that's who! Try to tell any of them—any of them!—that the tradition's just nonsense. Just try. *You* know it. *I* know it. I hope and trust that *Rory* knows it. But this entire benighted neighborhood is clinging to that last pathetic little shred of tradition as if it were the Union Jack!"

"That's very good," her grandfather noted approvingly. "The whole speech, in fact, but especially that last sentence."

Banner sank down in a chair across from his and put her head in her hands.

Jake smothered a laugh. "Now, lass—"

"Don't you 'now, lass' me!" she muttered, lifting her head and glaring at him. "You're matchmaking, dammit, and I won't have it! Or him!"

"Has he asked you to have him?" Jake asked dryly.

"I'm sure you'll manage to arrange *that* too!"

"I wouldn't think of it."

The events of a somewhat surprising and exhausting day had left Banner with her normal control in tatters, but she gathered what threads she could and calmed down. "Look," she said, carefully reasonable. "I know you're only trying to do what you think is best for me. But, Jake, I'm twenty-seven years old. I've fought the idea of selling the Hall, but I'm not stupid. If we have to sell, then we have to. You don't have to try and marry me to the man just to keep everything in the family!"

"It'd be the perfect solution, though," Jake mused wistfully. "Rory's obviously got a feeling for the place, and I'll bet he could turn it into a paying plantation in the first year."

Banner wasn't deceived by her grandfather's melancholy expression and words. "Fine," she said briefly. "Then take him on as a partner,

Jake; you run the place and he'll supply the capital."

Quite calmly, and with the utter determination that defies argument, Jake responded, "I'll sell it outright or leave it to you. Period."

"I can't afford it," she said, equally flat. "And you were right—I'd rather see you sell than watch the Hall crumble."

Jake was silent for a long moment, apparently weighing the strength of determination revealed in green eyes as stubborn as his own. Then he sighed and nodded. "All right, lass. I'll stop meddling. If anyone asks, I'll say that the last dance was an old man's joke. And we'll see if Rory makes an offer for the place."

It had been easier than she'd expected, but Banner abruptly felt depressed and tired. "We both know he will. Are you riding tomorrow? I mean today?"

"Of course I am. So I'd better get some sleep." Jake rose, looking down at his granddaughter and adding gently, "You should too."

"I think I'll find something to read," she

murmured restlessly. "I'm not very sleepy. Good night, Grandfather."

He bent to kiss the top of her head. "Good night, lass."

Banner watched him leave the room. She sat silently for a moment, thinking, remembering, then rose with a frown and went over to a particular section of the bookshelves. She found what she wanted quickly and carried the leather-bound book over to the rug in front of the banked and glowing fire. She stretched out on the thick white rug—her grandfather's single concession to taste rather than strict restoration in this room—and began searching through the book.

It was a privately printed volume written half a century before by a Clairmont—about Jasmine Hall. Banner impatiently thumbed through the chapters dealing with architecture and people, pausing only once as it occurred to her, belatedly and wrenchingly, that the Clairmont name, at least as concerned the Hall, would die with Jake. She shook the thought away firmly and continued to scan chapter headings. Ah—there it was, just as she'd remembered.

Ghosts and Legends.

Raised up on her elbows, her feet kicking absently in the air, Banner read carefully, scanning some passages and paying close attention to others. The author had possessed, in addition to natural family interest, a talent for writing, and he'd done his research; every legend Banner could remember hearing from the inexhaustible Jake was set down here in detail.

The soldiers and their brides—seen only by those who would live their lives at Jasmine Hall.

Banner frowned. She'd seen them, if not in the ballroom, then certainly upstairs in the hallway. They'd been hazy, to be sure, but she *had* seen them. She read on.

And here was...Oh. She didn't remember that part. "It is believed that if the soldiers and their brides dance the final dance at the ball with a betrothed couple, they are signifying their approval." Banner frowned again. "Damn their approval," she muttered, and continued reading.

She was looking for one item in particular, a vague memory nudging her, and found it at last.

The blond man.

He had not, she read in some surprise, been a Clairmont at all, but the "beau" of a Clairmont daughter. Killed in a hunting accident—and not even on Jasmine Hall property—he'd apparently chosen to spend eternity in the home of his beloved.

"I wonder if she married somebody else?" Banner questioned softly, making a note to look it up later, while irrepressible thoughts of awkward honeymoons came to mind.

According to the accepted legend, the blond beau had taken it upon himself to watch over all succeeding Clairmont daughters. He was often seen by other suitors, family, and friends though almost never seen by the girls themselves. And the only times he had been seen by the girls . . .

Banner read the last little bit with another frown, remarking firmly to the silent room, "Well, I won't be seeing you, if that's the case. And I hope your guardianship stops at my bedroom door!" Given the time in which he'd lived, she felt pretty certain that the beau would never think of crossing the threshold of a lady's bedroom.

Having found all she'd wanted, Banner leafed through the remainder of the book idly, her thoughts far away. She remained in her comfortable position, her green nightshirt enveloping her, feet kicking absently. And it was some minutes later that she felt a peculiar prickling sensation and knew that she was no longer alone in the room.

She'd become accustomed to the Jasmine Hall spirits long ago, often being conscious of them even when she couldn't see them; but Banner had been a bit unnerved by reading the confirmation of Rory's casual and unknowing observations. So she felt a little fierce when she abruptly turned her head to examine the room in search of a ghost.

There was absolute silence for a moment, broken only by her unconscious gasp. And for the second time that evening, she tried an unconcerned laugh that didn't quite come off. "Oh—it's you!"

Rory came forward to sit in the chair closest to her. "Sorry if I startled you," he said quietly.

He was dressed casually, but not for sleep, in jeans and a gray shirt open at the throat, and looked as restless as she felt. And his next words confirmed it.

"Couldn't sleep. Looks like we had the same idea," he added, nodding at the book still open in front of her.

Banner was glad he couldn't see the title, which was stamped in gold across the front of the book; she didn't know how Rory felt regarding ghosts, but she didn't really feel up to probing his thoughts on the subject tonight. "I was about to go up to bed," she lied uncomfortably.

Rory smiled just a little. "Is it the book or the company making you leave?" he asked.

Sighing, Banner sat up, tugging the lopsided neckline of her sleep shirt up over a shoulder and entirely unconscious of the provocative gesture.

She was nothing if not honest, and her attention was focused on the need to explain a few things. "Look, I apologize for Jake's little trick tonight. He should have explained about the dance when you asked to take his place. I'm afraid his sense of humor gets a little strange sometimes."

"He backed me rather neatly into a corner, didn't he?" Rory mused, his voice light but his gray eyes intent on the intriguing picture she made half-silhouetted by the fire behind her.

Banner shook her head instantly. "No, of course he didn't. Even though the neighborhood may have implicit faith in that old tradition, we're hardly living in times when things like that matter. We'll treat it as a joke and leave it at that, all right?"

Being an intelligent and prudent man, Rory thought it politic to agree. "Fine by me." Then he promptly spoiled his attempt at disinterest. "That nightshirt—or whatever it is—certainly puts you squarely in modern times, anyway."

She tugged again at the slipping neckline, this

time very conscious of the gesture. "From the sublime to the ridiculous," she offered lightly.

"Hardly ridiculous," Rory murmured. "If Rhett had caught Scarlett wearing something like that, he would have kidnapped her, instead of wasting all that time being patient."

Banner had the peculiar feeling that something was happening, and that it was happening too fast for her to control. She was neither too young nor too blind to mistake the desire in the gray eyes watching her so intently, but she was too much like her grandfather not to question this near-stranger's motives. "Look, just because Jake thinks he's living in the Middle Ages doesn't mean that you have to—"

"Have to?" Rory came down beside her on the rug, not thinking very much about Jake's wishes at the moment. "You're right—I have to. Ever since you opened the front door, I've wanted to."

And he did.

Banner had been kissed before. In fact, if the clock had really been turned back and focused on the antebellum South, she would have been considered the belle of the area. But Banner, her heart kept by her grandfather, Jasmine Hall, and her "hobby," painting, had tended to keep men at arm's length. She was friendly, but too briskly matter-of-fact to encourage even the lightest of romances. She'd even wondered once or twice if it was *possible* for her to feel anything stronger than mild interest in a man.

Now she knew. It was possible.

And possibility turned to reality left her confused and with the dizzying sensation of riding the rapids of some monster river on a flimsy raft.

She was stingingly aware of his hands on her shoulders, one clothed and one bare, and of the abrupt fierce hardening of his lips on hers. Dimly, she was conscious of her heart pounding in her ears, of the softness of the rug beneath her knees, of the strength of his thigh pressed against hers.

A suspicious part of her wanted to push him away and proclaim that she wouldn't be part of a package deal including Jasmine Hall or any kind of an inducement for a sale. That same part of her demanded that she splendidly ignore this obvious attempt to pander to an old man's wishes.

But she couldn't seem to push him away or say anything. She even felt a sense of satisfaction rather than surprise when she realized that her fingers had buried themselves in his thick silvery hair. She felt hot, but couldn't blame it on the fire behind her, and the restlessness she'd barely felt before, now tortured her.

Rory had completely forgotten both Jake's matchmaking and the possibility that this woman in his arms could have reason to question his motives. He hadn't questioned his own motives very closely, obeying without thought the driving urge to hold her, to be close to her.

But now, at her response, he felt something stir inside of him, a caged and sleeping beast awakened to prowl restlessly. And since he'd been unaware of its existence until this moment, the sudden awakening caught him completely by surprise. If he had ever vaguely questioned the notion of the "primitive" soul every man was supposed to possess, it had certainly been no more than a dim and brief question, and hardly prepared him for the emergence of his own passionate and possessive beast.

No other woman had ever touched fire to that deeply buried fuse. He had never felt such an abrupt and fierce hunger tempered and strengthened by a tenderness he'd thought himself incapable of. Desire warred with gentleness, need with sensitivity, and possessiveness with the innate understanding that no man had the right to possess a woman as if she were an object.

Two million years of instinct clashed with a sensitive intellect and left Rory reeling in the wake.

Banner chose that moment to pull away, scrambling to her feet and retreating to put a chair between them. She was breathing quickly and unevenly, and her face was white beneath the summer tan.

Rory got to his feet slowly, feeling curiously bereft, knowing that he was as pale as she.

"I...won't be part of a package deal," she said unsteadily.

She was staring at him, an odd, vulnerable little quiver to her lower lip. Rory had never considered himself psychic or even overly intuitive, but that little quiver told him in a flash that his future happiness was very much at stake and hinged entirely on whatever he said and did next.

He'd never in his life had to defuse a bomb, but Rory knew in that moment exactly what it felt like to do so. And the violent desire he felt for her abruptly channeled itself into rationality. His voice emerged, startling him with his own spontaneous, unthinking honesty.

"My mother is an honest-to-God Southern lady, and raised me to be a gentleman—as odd as that sounds in these modern times. She taught me several things I've had cause to be thankful for."

Banner stirred very slightly, the quiver still present. "Such as?" Her voice was almost inaudible.

"To be kind to little old ladies, patient with children, and good to animals." His voice was gentle and solemn and held no mockery. "To be gracious in victory as well as defeat. To respect the law, women, and my elders, and to think twice before disagreeing with any of them. To avoid lying, cheating, or losing my temper. And never to mix business and pleasure."

Banner was smiling faintly, her eyes still uncertain, but the vulnerable quiver was gone. And Rory was glad about that; it hurt him to see her vulnerable. He chose each word carefully now.

"I've always thought the . . . the worst dishonesty of all was to use personal means to achieve business goals. I've never done that, Banner. I don't intend to start now."

"You want the Hall." The words seemed almost forced from her.

"I want the Hall," he confirmed steadily. "And, not to put too fine a point on it, I want you," he added with utter calm. "But I'm not after a package deal, and I've never been one to cater to the whims of an old matchmaker just because I want to buy his house."

Banner studied him for a long moment. "I'm not so sure I trust you," she said finally, her tone wry. "You're just a bit too ready with the right words."

"Who knows what evil lurks in the hearts of men?" he intoned solemnly.

"Quit it," she ordered, a smile of genuine amusement tugging at her lips. And, as easily as that, the atmosphere between them was no longer thick with tension.

He grinned at her. "I'll call Mom and have her furnish a testimonial," he offered.

"Don't bother. She'd be prejudiced anyway."

"You don't know my mother," Rory said ruefully. "She's brutally honest, and underneath that smooth veneer of southern charm beats the heart of a termagant." He reflected for a moment. "She'd like you."

Banner frowned. "Are you drawing a comparison?"

"Oh, you noticed that?"

"I am not a termagant!"

"You were during the tour."

She had the grace to look slightly sheepish. "Sorry about that."

"Exercising your sword arm?" he wondered innocently.

"And if I was?"

"Well, feel free to exercise whenever you like," he offered generously. "My upbringing, you know; I'm too polite to hit a lady."

"I noticed that."

"Points in my favor?" he asked, hopeful.

Banner ignored his question. "I've picked out a hunter for you," she said conversationally. "I hope you'll be satisfied with him."

With a faint smile, Rory accepted the change of subject. "I'm sure I will. Exactly what kind of hunt is it, by the way?"

"A fox hunt."

"A real one?"

She shook her head. "Not really; Jake doesn't approve of killing animals for sport. Scottie—he takes care of the horses—will go out at dawn tomorrow and set up a trail, using a tame fox that belongs to one of our neighbors. At the end of the trail, he'll put an old stuffed fox from the attic up in a tree. The dogs don't seem to know the difference," she added cheerfully.

"What if a real fox wanders onto the trail?" Rory wondered.

"It's happened a couple of times before. When the dogs treed the fox, Scottie put them on their leashes and dragged them back to the house. The fox seemed more mad than afraid."

Before Rory could respond, the grandfather clock in the corner announced the hour in the whirring, rasping sound of gallant old age, and Banner sent it a startled look.

"Three o'clock! And I have to be up by eight." She realized quite suddenly that she could hardly hold her eyes open; the long day topped by bewildering emotions had totally drained her. "I have to go to bed." She looked at Rory. "The hunt starts at ten; breakfast is served from eight on."

He nodded. "Good night, Banner."

She felt herself flush beneath the warmth of his look, and beat a hasty retreat, murmuring an almost inaudible "Good night."

After she'd gone, Rory absently bent to retrieve the book she'd left on the rug. He stood turning it in his hands, staring toward the doorway. Then he sighed, placed the book on the mantel, and was halfway to the stairs before a niggling sense of something left undone sent him back to the library. But when he'd crossed back to the fireplace, he found the mantel bare of anything except ornaments. He frowned for a moment, muttered aloud to the empty room, "I'm half asleep," and headed resolutely for his room.

The room that still smelled elusively of jasmine.

Rory woke with the strong scent of jasmine tickling his nose, coming fully awake when he sneezed violently. Sliding out of bed and pulling on a robe, he conducted yet another search of his pleasant room. No flowers anywhere. Nothing, in fact, that smelled remotely like jasmine. Yet the scent was present, elusive but definitely there. Rory sneezed again, frowing as the scent seemed to grow stronger. He'd never noticed an allergic reaction to any type of flower before, but this jasmine scent was definitely bothering him now.

And where on earth was the scent coming from? Although the estate was called Jasmine Hall, he'd yet to see a sign of that particular flower.

He went to the window and raised the sash, deciding that he was taking his responsibilities as a polite guest to extremes; he'd have to speak to Banner or Jake and explain the apparent allergy. Perhaps the maids used air freshener, and what better than jasmine?

Half-sitting on the low sill and breathing in the crisp morning air, Rory glanced down at the rose garden and saw Banner. She was dressed in what must have been an antebellum riding costume, complete with hat, and had what appeared to be gloves and a riding whip tucked into her belt. She was sitting on a stone bench scattering food for the dozens of birds gathered all around her; obviously a usual morning ritual.

And she wasn't alone.

Rory frowned irritably as he stared at the blond man seated beside Banner on the bench. He couldn't tell if they were talking, but the man seemed pleased with the companionship.

Still frowning, Rory got up and went to his closet, searching to find the costume provided for him.

Fifteen minutes later he was leaving the house through the French doors and making his way across the rose garden. He found Banner still on the bench, but alone now, and still feeding the birds—which scattered at his approach.

She looked up at him a bit shyly. "Good morning."

"Morning." Rory sat down beside her, adding more tersely than he'd intended, "Where's your friend?"

Banner looked blank for a moment, then her expression cleared. "I...uh, haven't seen him."

Rory fought a brief battle with his worst self

and lost. Silently, he pointed up to the window he'd left raised.

She followed his gesture, then looked back at his face, apparently understanding what he meant. "You saw him?" she ventured.

"I saw him," Rory confirmed impatiently, puzzled by what seemed to be suppressed amusement in the expression on her face. "Look, I know you told me he wasn't 'that kind' of friend, and God knows I've no right to question you, but it bothers me. Why does he keep running off whenever I'm around? Who is he? And what is he to you?"

Startled, Banner identified jealousy in his tone. She tried not to think about what that meant, concentrating instead on the realization that Rory was going to be suspicious anyway when the party was over, the guests gone, and he continued to see people dressed in something other than modern fashion. But she didn't think he'd believe her.

"His name," she murmured, "is Brett Andrews. At least, I think it is."

Rory blinked. "You think?"

"Uh-huh. We've . . . we've never met formally."

"If you don't want me to know," Rory stated with extreme politeness, "then don't tell me."

Banner decided that she had a choice of either further offending Rory with evasiveness or shocking him with the truth. She sighed. "Rory, I've never seen this man."

"What? He was sitting beside you!"

"I didn't see him."

"*I* saw him. From my window. And I saw him yesterday."

"I'm sure you did."

He stared at her, noting that she'd dispensed with the ringlet-dressed wig and wore her hat at a rakish angle. He watched her rubbing the bridge of her nose in an odd, rueful little gesture. And he saw the gravity behind the laughter in her sea-green eyes. "What're you telling me?" he asked carefully.

"That you saw a ghost."

"I don't believe in ghosts."

Banner ignored the instant, flat denial. Conversationally, she said, "I won't say that the Hall is haunted, because that implies chains rattling in the night and footsteps on the stairs and cold spots in certain rooms. We're not really *haunted*, it's just that most of the family decided to... stay."

"You don't expect me to believe that," he said incredulously.

She smiled a little. "It's up to you. I just wanted you to be prepared, because when the guests leave today and you go on seeing people dressed peculiarly...Well, I wanted you to know."

"Banner, I *saw* the man as clearly as I saw you." He stared at her. "Are you putting me on?"

"No."

"Ghosts?"

"Ghosts. Don't worry," she added encouragingly. "You'll get used to them. They're very *nice* ghosts."

"I can't deal with this," Rory said definitely.

She giggled. "Sorry. I suppose it's true that we

Americans aren't as blasé about ghosts as the Europeans, because we haven't had as much history to produce them. But there's a lot of history in Jasmine Hall, and family feeling has always been very strong here."

Rory smiled wryly, not quite believing but not sure enough to *dis*believe, either. "The blond man?"

"According to legend, he guards—as ridiculous as it sounds—the young ladies of the house."

"And you've never seen him?"

"No. That's part of the legend too. After you saw him yesterday, I looked it up, because I only half-remembered that story."

"Looked it up?"

"In the Jasmine Hall book. A Clairmont with literary talents wrote everything up and had it privately printed, ghosts and all."

"I'd like to read it."

Banner nodded agreeably. "I'll get it for you later. I was looking through it last night when you came into the library."

Rory thought of the night before, and of the book that had not long remained on the mantel, where he'd left it. He decided, somewhat uncomfortably, not to mention that to Banner.

"Have you had breakfast?" she was asking prosaically.

"No, how about you?"

"Not yet. Shall we?" She rose from the bench.

Following suit, Rory suddenly remembered something. "Oh, by the way—I don't mean to complain, but could we do something about the scent of jasmine in my room? It must be air freshener, or something; I couldn't find anything else. I wouldn't mind, but I seem to have a slight allergy and woke up sneezing this morning."

Banner was staring at him. "Jasmine?" she said in an odd voice.

"Yes." He looked at her curiously, wondering.

She turned rather abruptly and headed across the garden toward the house. "Of course. I'll— see what we can do."

She was laughing inside, but decided sympathetically not to heap yet another ghost on

Rory's bewildered head. Because she was reasonably sure that the scent he spoke of wasn't a product of this world, but another one.

Her mother had loved jasmine, and had worn the scent always.

FOUR

FROM THE VANTAGE point of the back of a tall gray Thoroughbred, Rory watched riders assembling for the hunt. As Banner had predicted, most of the guests had seemed a bit sheepish at breakfast, but they were back on balance now, and the Grand Old South was once more at the forefront of things.

Currier and Ives would have loved the scene.

Yelping beagles wandered restlessly among the horses, never too far away from the redheaded middle-aged man Banner had introduced as Scottie; he was clearly adored by all the animals. Ladies in colorful riding habits coped easily with troublesome sidesaddles and spirited horses. Gentlemen talked and laughed.

In the background were the barns, three long ones surrounding an open area where the horses and riders were milling about. The stabling was adequate, Rory thought musingly, for all the horses—those belonging to Jasmine Hall and those sent here days ago by the guests who wanted to ride their own. Rory's experienced eye detected pure-blooded, expensive Thoroughbreds comprising those animals sporting the red browband on their bridles that proclaimed them as belonging to the Hall. His own gray gelding was as sleek and well trained as any he'd seen in major show-rings.

Then his attention was caught once more by the spectacle of Jasmine Hall turned out for the hunt.

"Amazing, isn't it?" Banner had ridden her black gelding up beside Rory and now controlled his prancing with an experienced hand. "You'd think somebody had turned back the clock."

"You'd think," he agreed, glancing once more at the scene around them and then gazing at her. "How d'you manage the sidesaddle?"

She laughed. "It's easy once you've learned how. Balance is everything."

"I can imagine. Does that brute realize he's carrying a lady?"

Banner frowned at him and bent forward to stroke the glossy black neck of her mount. "Don't call El Cid a brute. I raised him and trained him myself."

Rory watched the huge horse prance in place as though he were performing for judges in a dressage event, noting that Banner seemed as comfortable as she would have been on solid ground. "El Cid? He was a Spanish national hero, wasn't he?"

"Uh-huh. But it's the literal meaning of the name that I love—'the lord.' Fits, doesn't it?"

"He is lordly," Rory admitted. "And what's mine called?"

Banner smiled serenely at him. "Shadow."

He looked at her suspiciously, but Banner maintained an innocent expression. Rory sighed. "Right. I really don't know if I want to hear the answer, but—will any of the Hall...uh, spirits ride today?"

"I've never seen any," she responded gravely.

"That doesn't comfort me."

Banner laughed suddenly. "If you see one, just tip your hat in passing."

"You should ask one of 'em to sit for you," he told her firmly. "I doubt that any other artist has captured a ghost—from the flesh, so to speak."

Before she could respond, Scottie signaled the beginning of the hunt, his long horn echoing in the morning air. The dogs moved toward the meadow, casting about for the scent, and almost instantly gave tongue in their loud, eerily plaintive voices.

The hunt was on.

Rory had ridden all his life, and he was familiar with steeplechase-type courses made hazardous by wicked jumps and a fast and constant pace, but he had never experienced an honest-to-goodness hunt.

His respect for these apparently leisurely ladies and gentlemen increased enormously as the morning wore on. They handled their mounts easily, and all rode with the certain comfort of those almost literally born in the saddle. Not a single guest was unseated—and the jumps were wicked.

Banner and Jake, Rory noticed, kept right in the thick of things. It was those two, she on her El Cid and her grandfather on a deep-chested, long-legged white gelding, who showed their guests the way over brush, rail, and water. It might have been an amiable competition between them or merely the hard-riding nature of their heritage; whatever the reason, they were nearly always neck-and-neck in the lead.

The false trail led them for miles over the countryside, across streams and meadows and through forests, and it wasn't until they had experienced the "kill" and watched the hounds leashed at the base of a large tree where a stuffed fox glared mockingly down on them that Rory was able to come up alongside Banner. All the riders had turned their mounts back toward Jasmine Hall at a leisurely pace.

"That," Rory said definitely, "was something to remember."

Cheeks flushed and green eyes merry, Banner nodded agreement. "There are hunt clubs around here that run hunts from time to time, but we're the only ones who're costumed. It adds something, doesn't it?"

"It does that." He looked over their horses, noting the damp sheen of sweat but also aware that neither animal—clearly well conditioned— was overly tired. "Do we have time to ride over more of the property, or should you return with your guests?"

Abruptly, the light left her eyes. "No, I don't have to get back right away. I can show you the southern section, at least. This way." She turned

El Cid away from the rest of the horses, heading in a direction the hunt hadn't covered.

Rory was silently cursing himself. He brought Shadow alongside her horse again. "Banner, I'm sorry."

She sent him a quick glance. "It's all right; Jake can take care of the guests."

"That isn't what I meant, and you know it." He sighed. "You were so happy about the hunt, and I had to spoil your pleasure by reminding you that I came here to look the place over. I'm sorry."

The horses were walking, and Banner had little need to pay close attention to her riding; still, she didn't look at him. "Well, it's the reason you're here. And . . . Jake's serious this time." She smiled faintly. "It probably isn't good salesmanship—by Jake's way of thinking—to tell you that, but it's true."

He was silent for a moment. "D'you have to sell?" It was, perhaps, spiking his own guns, since he wanted the place, but Rory was troubled by her obvious grief at losing Jasmine Hall.

Banner shrugged. "We can't afford to keep it in prime condition; you know what restoration and maintenance cost these days. It's either turn the place over to a historical society or sell."

"And it'll kill you to have to leave here." It wasn't a question, and the rough tone told her more, perhaps, than he'd intended.

She stared straight ahead between Cid's alert ears. "I'll survive."

There was silence for a while, broken only by morning sounds and the muffled thuds of hooves. Rory saw the land they rode through, but he didn't really look at it. He was peculiarly conscious of the costume he wore and of the costumed lady by his side, bemusedly aware that while his instincts might have sparked action because they were alone, the manners curiously imposed by the costumes forbade it.

He would, he realized, be glad when the costumes were packed away for—what? Next year? Or would there be a next year for this hunt?

Shunting the thought aside, he asked abruptly, "Is Jake your only family?"

"He is now. My father was killed in a car accident when I was just a child. Mother died ten years ago. There are aunts, uncles, and cousins scattered around the country, but it's just been Jake and me for years."

"What are your future plans if the Hall is sold?" He hated to keep reminding her, but he was more than a little interested in anything that had to do with Banner's future.

She sent him a sudden look that was surprise overlaid by sadness. "It's funny, but I haven't thought that far ahead. I doubt that Jake has either. We were both born here; there's always been the Hall for us." Then she shrugged, and her voice lightened with a clear effort. "I suppose we'll buy a small place somewhere with a bit of land; neither of us could bear living in a city or even in an apartment. But that isn't your problem, Rory," she finished firmly.

"Isn't it?" He stared straight ahead, suddenly angry about the entire situation. He wanted the Hall, but not at the price of depriving Banner and Jake of a much-loved home; and knowing that they had no choice but to sell to *someone* helped not one bit. He was angry because the costumed ball and hunt would inevitably become nothing more than a sliver of local history; the tightly-knit neighborhood here would hardly care to see the Hall family tradition turned into little more than an interesting game for tourists-guests. He was angry because, for the first time, a piece of property seemed like a home to him rather than a money-making proposition, and the thought of careless tourists tramping through its gracious halls actually sickened him.

And he was angry because he very badly wanted to become a part of Banner's life—and the Hall loomed between them. If he bought the plantation, would he always be the man who'd taken away her home, however gently he managed the transaction? Even if he kept the place for his own home—an idea that appealed strongly to him, however impractical it might be—it would no longer belong to Banner's family. And if he decided not to buy, it would only force Jake either to offer it to someone else, someone with no scruples or interest in the family, or to turn it over to a historical society.

It was a no-win situation.

Banner knew that he was angry; the emotion was obvious from his grim expression and troubled eyes. And because she was slowly getting to know this man, she understood the source of his anger. His feeling for these old plantations and his deepening interest in this particular family held him trapped in an unenviable position. He wasn't the type of man to walk away from the problem, to disassociate himself from the future of Jasmine Hall just so that he wouldn't be responsible for whatever happened.

Quietly, she said, "You want the Hall. You don't have to see the rest of the property, do you?"

Rory sighed, and his voice was rough when he answered. "I want the Hall. But I don't want anything to change. Not for the Hall—and not for you and Jake. I want there to be a ball and a hunt every year, where the neighbors revert and celebrate the glory of the Grand Old South. I want to watch Southern gents threatening to duel in the garden and I want to listen to debates on the presidency of Mr. Lincoln. I want to know that there's still a traditional midnight waltz at Jasmine Hall."

Banner swallowed hard, almost unbearably moved by the muted passion in his deep voice. He was not giving lip service to what he thought she wanted to hear; he *felt* the same aching love for this very special home of hers that she did. It came to her then that only a special man with deep sensitivity could have become so very involved so quickly.

For the first time, she *wanted* him to have the Hall. He would take care of her home if she couldn't do it herself.

She wasn't aware that the horses had responded to tense hands on their reins by halting, until she looked around. They were standing at the edge of a clearing in the woods where a small brook murmured softly to itself in the shaded quiet. Banner forced herself to ignore her tight throat and to speak briskly.

"Then you'll buy the place, of course. Unless Jake's price is totally outrageous. You'll buy the place," she repeated softly, trying to accustom herself to the sound of that. "Change is a part of life, Rory; you aren't responsible for the fact that Jake's and my lives have to change."

"Am I not?" His voice was grim. "Then how will you feel, Banner, after I've taken your home away from you? How will you feel about me?"

Banner signaled El Cid to move forward, and as the horse responded obediently, she tried to answer him. "I don't know. But I'm not a child, Rory; I know someone has to buy the Hall. I'd— rather it was you. And . . . that's all."

He guided his horse to follow as she turned back toward the house, realizing that she'd given him the only answer she could at this point. But he knew, with a sinking feeling, what her eventual answer would be. Jasmine Hall was not a house, and not merely a home; it was a part of Banner. And no matter how gracious this innately *Southern* lady would be over the loss of that, it would never be forgotten.

She would forgive him for what he would have to do to her. But she would never be able to forget.

The merry lunch was over. The guests were gone, the horses stabled for a night's rest before those belonging to the guests would be trailered or ridden home. Banner had vanished to her room, silent, troubled, withdrawn. And Rory changed from his costume before leaving his own, still-scented room.

He wandered for a while, restless, his mind working keenly but finding no solution. He heard Jake's voice once and deliberately took a hallway angling away from that sound; he didn't want to talk to the older man just yet.

He wanted to think.

Rory knew now why the idea of depriving Banner of a home was so painful to him. He had known since he'd heard the jealousy in his own voice that morning when he'd been confronted with what he'd feared to be a rival. It had been a shock to him to realize what he felt for Banner was much more than simple desire.

Dear God, so quickly? He didn't know why it had happened—not specifically. If asked, he could only have pointed to absurd little things brought into focus by his bemused mind. The vulnerable little quiver of her lower lip. The way she rubbed her nose in a rueful, unconscious gesture. The drawling lilt in her voice. The sight of a Southern lady riding sidesaddle on a prancing horse named El Cid.

Unseeing, Rory stopped in the middle of the hallway, his gaze fixed absently on a painting hanging on the wall. He couldn't, he knew, bear to be the man who took her home away from her. Nor could he disclaim responsibility and walk away, leaving her future and that of Jasmine Hall unresolved. He wanted to be a part of her future, but would *she* want that after losing her home?

She didn't want to be a part of a package deal. Her pride. He couldn't blame her for that. What would she say if he said, "Marry me and live with me here at the Hall"?

She could say any number of things. She could attribute the proposal to a guilty conscience—and say no. She could think that he'd chosen to forego his mother's advice and mix business and pleasure—and say no. She could decide quite realistically that she hardly knew him—and say no. She could wear her pride like her name and vanish from his life—without even saying no.

Rory swore softly, tonelessly. Boxed in, trapped. Damned, no matter what he did. After a long moment, his unseeing gaze sharpened. His mind churned violently, then settled down. Rapidly, he considered his sudden thought. Would it work? Maybe. It was a chance. His one chance.

He swung around and went quickly down the hall, heading for the front door. Couldn't use the phone here. Might be overheard, and it wouldn't do to let anyone in on his idea until he was sure it would work. She'd probably be mad as hell even if it *did* work—at first, anyway.

He'd have to chance it.

"Rory?" Jake, coming out of the library, was clearly startled to see his guest making for the front door as if he were being chased by something large and carnivorous.

"I have to go to town for something," Rory explained rapidly without explaining a thing and not pausing for a reply.

Jake stared rather blankly at the door as it closed behind his guest. His keen eyes cleared after a moment. "Wonder what that boy's up to?" he murmured to himself thoughtfully.

"Are you talking to me, Jake?" Banner was coming down the stairs.

"Hmmm?" He looked at her. "Oh—no, lass. To myself." Having already been on the receiving end of a lecture from Rory on the merits of keeping his nose out of other people's business in general and his granddaughter's in particular, Jake decided to keep his speculation to himself. He'd seen which way the wind blew, and was content to allow the younger man to manage his own affairs. It would most likely be very interesting—to say the least.

"Where's Rory?" she asked lightly.

"He had to go to town for something," Jake reported faithfully. "I'm sure he'll be back soon."

Banner was too preoccupied to notice her grandfather's overly innocent tone; her mind was on something else. "Jake, this morning Rory mentioned a slight problem with his room."

"Which is?"

She leaned against the newel post and stared at him wryly. "The scent of jasmine. He thinks he may be allergic to it."

"The scent of— Oh. Well, well."

"It's not funny, Jake."

"Tell Sarah that."

"I'm more interested in what we're going to tell Rory. How am I going to explain to him about Mother? Especially when I don't know what she's up to."

"She's obviously keeping an eye on him."

"But why?"

Jake looked at her guilelessly. "Could be she's interested because he wants the Hall."

"I suppose." Banner was faintly dissatisfied, but resigned. "Anyway, what do I tell Rory?"

"The truth."

"Jake, I've told him about the blond man and I've mentioned that there are others. He isn't going to be happy when I explain that my mother—who happens to be a ghost—is visiting him and drenching his room with the jasmine scent."

The old man shrugged and spread his hands helplessly. "Then just ignore the subject and hope it doesn't come up again," he suggested.

"You're a lot of help."

"Sorry."

Banner shelved the problem for the time being and headed for her cottage studio. She had a great many things on her mind, and work had always helped her to think. However, once in her studio with brush and palette in hand, she found that her work in progress did little to distract her from thinking about Rory.

Twenty-four hours, and the man was becoming an obsession with her.

She frowned at the portrait of a blond gentleman. Rory had assumed the painting to be of her "friend." When he had taken a closer look, he'd seen only similarities between it and himself.

But the portrait *was* of Rory. It was he, and she'd never laid eyes on him when she'd begun it.

Now, however, she found herself deliberately and consciously painting from her mental image of Rory. And from more than her *mental* image. She tried to paint blond hair that was silky soft to the touch. She tried to paint the feeling of strong arms beneath smooth material. She tried to convey that firm, curved lips felt like warm satin. . . .

When she realized what she was doing, what she was feeling, Banner hastily laid the palette aside, swearing softly.

"Dead end," she said aloud in the still room. "No matter how . . . how interested he is, it's a dead end. I'd always wonder which was more important to him: me or the Hall. I'd always wonder if he wanted one because it was a part of the other. He won't walk away. He'll buy the place. And after I leave...what will I have?"

She knew what she'd have. Nothing. She was trained for nothing except managing a large house. Painting was a hobby, but could she fill her time with only that? With no vast home to manage, no century-old garden to tend lovingly...what then?

Banner was a practical woman. There could be other gardens. There could be a smaller house to manage. She and Jake were hardly destitute; it wasn't as if she would be cast out penniless into a cold world.

But her *place* would be gone. It was selfish, she knew; the most important thing was to preserve the Hall. No longer as her Hall, though. No longer her home.

And then there was Rory. He was clearly sensitive to the fact that his buying the place would uproot her. They had only...only a beginning. A sense of *simpatia*. Of understanding. A desire she didn't deceive herself into thinking was not mutual. Shared humor.

What would happen to them? He had posed the question bluntly: "What will you think of me when I've taken your home away from you?"

After a scant twenty-four hours, she knew that Rory could become important to her. Left to themselves, with no pressure from plantations or decisions, he could become vitally important to her.

And she wanted that.

But how *would* she feel about him when he took over the home that was in her blood? Whether he turned the Hall into a guest resort or lived in it himself—which was, she thought, likely—how would she feel? She thought of her grandfather's blatantly obvious desire to marry her off to Rory, a man who could afford to maintain the plantation until he could turn it into a paying concern in some way, and winced.

Were that unlikely event to take place, wouldn't she always wonder? Wouldn't she always think, at some deep level within herself, that Rory had taken the easiest way out? Assuming he would want to marry her, of course. Marry the girl and get the house as well...

Automatically, Banner cleaned her brushes and scraped the palette. She reminded herself silently, fiercely, that the point was moot. There would be no future with Rory, because all they would ever have would be this tantalizing beginning. It would stop there.

Jasmine Hall stood immovably between them.

She went to the house through the rose garden, as usual, pausing and taking a few moments to savor the scent and the colorful profusion of blooms. As she entered the vast entrance hall, she heard the sounds of voices coming from her grandfather's library; then, when she was farther along, she noticed that the door was ajar, even as she recognized Rory's deep voice.

"Like I said, Jake, ask me no questions and I'll tell you no lies. Just accept that I know what I'm doing. Do I get the favor?"

Jake replied, clearly amused and faintly puzzled. "You get the favor. I won't ask any questions. But are you sure—?"

"I'm sure."

Before Banner could absorb the curious conversation, she was caught unintentionally eavesdropping when Rory strode briskly from the library. He didn't seem the slightest bit upset to find her there; instead, his face lit up in a way that caused her heart to leap alarmingly.

"There you are," he said cheefully. "I was wondering where you'd disappeared to."

Uncomfortably aware both of her eavesdropping and of the depressive lingering of her earlier thoughts, Banner's voice was a bit subdued when she answered. "I was in my studio. Um, I didn't mean to listen in, but you asked Jake for a favor?"

"More time," Rory told her firmly. "There's no great hurry, after all. Jake just agreed to give me time enough to think things over carefully."

Banner was torn. She was faintly resentful that he could be so cheerful at the thought of possibly buying her home; she felt an irrepressible surge of elation that whatever decision was to be made was still in the future. But she wondered... "Will you be staying?"

"If that's all right with you."

The suddenly gentle tone and intent gaze brought a flush to her cheeks in spite of all her efforts to control it. "Gentlemen give notice of loaded questions," she managed lightly, even though both of them knew it hadn't been a question.

He laughed, then looked her up and down quite thoroughly. "And ladies should give due warning whenever they're going to wear jeans and a T-shirt. Rhett *definitely* wouldn't have been patient."

Unconsciously, they had both wandered from the foyer and out into the rose garden. Banner wondered dimly why she suddenly felt as cheerful as he seemed to be, but decided not to probe too deeply into the matter. The pressures had been lifted—if only for the time being—and her nature was too optimistic to allow her to remain depressed for long.

"Thank you," she said gravely. "I assume that was a compliment."

"Don't fish," he chided severely, taking her hand in a casual way as they strolled along one of the paths.

"I was not fishing." She decided not to make an issue of this hand-holding business; he didn't seem aware of what he'd done anyway. Besides, she liked it.

"Are you kidding? I can see a hook when it's damn well dangled under my nose."

"Just because I didn't want blood in the rose garden last night," she warned, "doesn't mean I don't think it might do the plants some good this afternoon."

"All right, all right. I'll be a gentleman and pretend you weren't fishing."

"That graceful concession lacked something," she noted thoughtfully.

"Diplomacy, maybe?"

"I'd say."

"Sorry."

"Right. Um—listen. Are we going some-where?"

"We're walking in the rose garden, wench. Where's your sense of romance?"

Banner was a bit bemused by this Rory. He was definitely at odds with the troubled man of a couple of hours before, and a far cry from the cool, businesslike man of yesterday. It was a puzzle, but one she didn't really want to solve. She liked this cheerful, bantering man who held her hand absently and teased her. He seemed to have shed years and cares, and she was quite willing to postpone tomorrow.

"My sense of romance," she said solemnly, "is fine, thank you very much. I just wondered if we were going somewhere in particular, that's all."

He sent her an amused look, then changed the subject slightly. "Speaking of which, what say we plan a barbecue for next weekend?"

She blinked. "A barbecue?"

"Sure. I'll spring for it."

"What has that to do with romance?" she asked bemusedly.

"The delights of cooking, eating, and mingling under a starry sky aren't romantic?"

"Mingling?"

He rewarded her laughing query with a mock frown, then went on briskly. "We can start the thing in the late afternoon and go on till whenever. Invite the friends and business associates we have in town—I'm not exactly a stranger to these parts, you know. We'll have music and tons of good food and— There is a pool back behind the garden, isn't there? I thought I saw one this morning."

"There is a pool," she agreed.

"Terrific. We'll combine a barbecue with a pool party. I'm dying to see you in a swimsuit anyway."

Banner tried valiantly to ignore his last comment. "Well, I'm game. It'll take some arranging, though. Invitations, food, musicians, and so on. Is there any particular reason you want to have a party? We just finished one, as I recall."

"I told you. I want to see you in a swimsuit."

Very dryly, she said, "You don't have to drop a bundle on an expensive party for that reason. Whenever not occupied by parties, I tend to swim early every morning."

"I'll get up early tomorrow," he commented promptly.

Banner laughed, but shook her head. "None of this makes sense. However." She shrugged. "You've talked to Jake about the party?"

"Of course. That's the other part of my favor, as a matter of fact. He thinks it's a dandy idea."

"That's because he loves parties. Well, since you two have decided, I'll start making the arrangements."

"Sure you don't mind? I could make them."

"Oh, I don't mind. Just let me know whom to invite and how much to spend."

"Jake's working up a list of guests. And you have no budget, milady. Sky's the limit."

"You may regret that. In fact, I'm sure you will."

"I trust you not to bankrupt me." He grinned

down at her. "And I have a few touches of my own I'd like to discuss with you."

She mistrusted the grin. "Really? What kinds of touches?"

"You think an elephant would be too much?"

The solemn tone got her for a moment. She stopped dead in her tracks in front of a particularly beautiful Forty-niner rosebush and stared up at him. Then, seeing the glint in his gray eyes, she relaxed. "My God—I thought you were serious."

"A dog act, then?" he asked anxiously.

"Quit it."

He started laughing. "It was worth it to see your face. Come on, show me the pool and we'll start planning."

FIVE

THE NEXT FEW days were hectic ones. And peculiar. Raised in a family that traditionally loved parties, Banner was accustomed to planning quite lavish ones; Rory's barbecue-and-pool-party-cum-moonlight proved to be no exception.

Clearly determined that she not be forced to do all the work, he threw his energy—which was considerable—into the effort. They worked together companionably over lists, shared the chore of innumerable phone calls and errands, bickered amiably over what kind of music and who was to cater, and argued the merits of Japanese lanterns versus torches around the pool.

The Hall servants bore up nobly under the deluge of temporary help and delivery vans, although Conner, their butler, who had been given the prior week off to visit a sick relative, threatened to give notice when it turned out that the caterer Rory had hired was Creole and explosively temperamental.

Rory saved that situation, although Banner never could find out from the principals exactly *how* he managed. And she was desperately curious, because the normally taciturn Conner walked around for two days with a peculiarly shy smile on his face, and then tended to poker up whenever he saw her watching him.

"What on earth did you bribe the man with?"

"Shame on you. I'm above bribery."

"Oh, of course. Did you find him a hot date?"

"Banner!"

"That shocked look sits ill on your devious face."

"Just for that, I'll never tell you."

"Rory!"

One of Rory's "special touches" turned out to be a hayride, which he planned with meticulous detail. He managed to find six huge wagons, the teams to pull them, and a driver for each wagon. He found the sweetest-smelling hay in the county for the wagons. He even managed to locate an old rutted trail that wound for miles all around the plantation and never got near paved roads or the noisy sounds of civilization.

"The invitations look peculiar, you know."

"How so?"

"Well, explaining the moonlight barbecue and pool party is no problem, but how do I warn the guests to bring jeans for the hayride?"

"You say: Optional hayride—bring jeans."

"There's something lacking in that."

"Who's going to care?"

"True."

As the days slipped by, Banner was uneasily aware that Rory's companionship was becoming far too important to her. From their morning swim to a late snack before bedtime, they were almost constantly together. To be sure, it was an undemanding companionship; other than holding her hand or occasionally draping an arm around her shoulders, Rory made no attempt to put their relationship on a more intimate footing.

She told herself she was glad of that, told herself what was never begun could have no painful ending. She didn't believe herself.

She could at least partially put the matter out of her mind during the busy, laughter-filled days. But the nights were hell. It was more than irritating to one who had always slept easily and soundly to find herself suddenly restless and awake long into the night. She tried hot chocolate and warm baths, and she tried counting sheep. Nothing worked.

On Thursday, the night before the party, she was particularly restless. A week of being constantly in Rory's company, trying vainly to ignore the tense awareness his nearness brought, had taken its toll. It was late, the house was dark and quiet, and Banner lay awake staring at a shadowy ceiling. The fifth time she looked at the clock on her nightstand, it was two A.M.

Deciding that it was better to be up and doing something if she must be awake, she threw back the covers and left the bed. After flipping a mental coin, she exchanged the sleep shirt for one of her swimsuits. She normally wore a relatively modest one-piece when she swam in the mornings, but this time chose a daring bikini she never wore unless she was sure to be alone; it was her "tanning suit," purchased simply because it was the briefest thing she had been able to find.

She pulled a white terry beach caftan from her closet and drew it on, picked up a thick towel from her bathroom, then padded barefoot downstairs and through the silent house.

The day had been hot and still; the night was warm and a bit muggy. It was typical midsummer weather for the South, and the weather prediction promised another such day and night for their party. Banner automatically followed the garden path out to the pool. She stopped at the side of the cabana to flip the switch activating the underwater pool lights, then opened the gate and stepped inside the two-acre "privacy fence" that surrounded the pool.

It wasn't until she'd crossed several yards of sparkling tile that she realized she hadn't been the only one in the house with this idea.

"Hi," Rory called softly from the middle of the pool.

The underwater lights bathed the entire area in a hazy blue light, and between that and the full moon, she could see him clearly. He had spoken while floating lazily on his back, but now swam toward the side closest to her with the easy, powerful strokes she knew so well from their morning swims. Banner dropped her towel on a table and slid her hands into the deep pockets of her caftan, suddenly very conscious of the lateness of the hour and of the fact that they were more alone than they'd ever been. Even though they had shared the pool early every morning this past week, she had always been aware of the sounds of gardeners working to ready the area all around the pool for their party.

She didn't cross the remaining couple of feet of tile, but remained where she was. "Hi. I—I didn't think anyone else was still up."

"I've been out here every night about this time," he said calmly, resting his elbows and forearms on the tile as he gazed up at her.

"Every night? I didn't realize you liked swimming that much."

"What I *don't* like is staring at a dark ceiling. Come on in. The water's great."

Banner forced herself to ignore the implications of his first comment; he probably just meant he was a confirmed insomniac, that was all. At any rate, she was suddenly too busy remembering her scanty swimsuit to think about much else. She considered making some excuse to avoid entering the water, but knew that whatever she said, he'd think she was avoiding *him*.

If only he wouldn't keep *watching* her. Once in the water, her suit wouldn't look quite so brief, but standing here in full view of God and everybody—

"What's wrong?" Then, in a suddenly altered voice, he added, "I can leave if you'd rather swim alone."

"No. No, of course not." Banner walked to the edge of the pool at right angles to him, where wide steps led down into the shallow end. Trying to move as quickly as possible without looking as if she were hurrying, she pulled the long caftan up over her head, tossed it aside, and stepped down into the water.

She didn't look toward Rory, still at the side and utterly motionless, but instead struck out for the far end, swimming the length of the pool in her easy, graceful crawl. She swam back until her feet touched bottom in the shallow end, standing upright, so that the surface of the water came just to her breasts.

"You're right," she said breathlessly to the man who still hadn't moved. "The water is great."

"So's that suit."

Banner knew that it was hardly possible, anatomically speaking, for a heart to turn over; she wondered vaguely what actually happened to that organ to produce such a peculiar feeling. And she stood very still, because there had been something in his voice, an oddly taut, leashed quality, that warned her this moment was a dangerous one.

"Another thing that would have tried Rhett's patience," he added huskily.

Banner managed a shaky laugh. "I only wear it when I'm—when I think I'll be alone. For sunbathing."

He left the side, moving toward her until he stood just an arm's length away. "There's no sun now," he pointed out.

"But I thought I'd be alone."

"Don't ask me to leave."

It was half command and half plea. Banner found herself staring, almost hypnotized, at the broad expanse of his chest. It should have been unthreateningly familiar to her after a week of morning swims, but it seemed to her then that she'd never really looked before. Never really *let* herself look before. Now she saw the sleek, dark gold mat of hair covering tanned, muscled flesh, and swallowed hard.

"Rory, I—"

"Do you know," he interrupted, stepping even closer, "what I first noticed about you? Green eyes and an impossibly tiny waist. I thought: Scarlett O'Hara, for heaven's sake! But with you around, she'd never have been the belle of three counties."

"You're hung up on that book," she said with forced lightness.

"Parallels, I suppose." His voice was absent. One hand lifted to touch her cheek gently, then slid down to her throat, his thumb stroking her jawline. "Green eyes and a tiny waist. And the Hall's your Tara. But you're not in love with another man—are you?"

"No." She knew he could feel the pulse pounding in her neck, knew that her quick, shallow breathing was obvious to him. But she could only stare up at him, fascinated by the sparkling droplets of water adorning smooth golden skin. Fascinated by his deep voice, by the warmth of his hand. And she caught her breath audibly when his free hand found her waist beneath the water.

"I always thought," he mused softly, "that Rhett was misunderstood by everyone—not just Scarlett. He wanted her so badly, and waited so patiently for her to want him. And they came so close, those two. Do you think she got him back, by the way?"

Banner knew dimly that he was drawing more parallels, knew that he was telling her something. But her bemused mind just couldn't cope with cryptic ideas. Not then. So she answered his question. "Yes. She got him back."

"But he left her," Rory reminded softly. "He said he didn't give a damn what happened to her."

"He was tired. He was exhausted." Banner wasn't really listening to her own words; she just spoke instinctively. "But he loved her. He'd loved her for so long. He would have come back to her. He did come back to her."

Rory bent his head until his breath was warm on her face, and smiled slowly. "Your sense of romance is definitely fine, milady."

"Do—do you think he came back?" she murmured.

"I know he did."

Banner's eyes remained open, staring into the darkened slate gray of his; they seemed to fill her vision, her mind, velvety pools she wanted to drown herself in. His lips teased hers, brushing in a satiny caress that tempted her, tortured her. His tongue probed the sensitive inner flesh of her parted lips, sending shivers through her body.

His body was taut against hers, his tension evident when his hand moved to the small of her back and pressed her hips to his. But he made no

move to deepen the kiss. Instead, the tormenting, unsatisfying little caresses went on and on,
sapping her strength and willpower. His fingers
stroked her throat, the back of her neck, then
tangled in her thick curls to hold her head firmly.

Jerkily, her hands lifted to his chest, fingertips
exploring silky hair and firm flesh. She wanted
so badly to touch him, wanted so badly to feel
his strong arms locked around her body. Nothing else seemed to matter. Knowingly, willingly,
she closed her eyes and abandoned a fight that
had never begun.

Whether he sensed her feelings or simply lost
patience himself, Rory abruptly deepened the
kiss in fierce need. His mouth slanted across hers
hotly, desperately, drawing from her more than
she could afford to lose.

But Banner didn't care. Since the passionate
embrace of that first night and during all the casual touches of the past week, hunger had built
within her like floodwaters behind a dam. She
was lost in the swirling rush of escaping passion,
afloat only because he held her. Her arms slid

around his neck, and the feeling of his arms locked around her body fed the hunger inside her.

The warm water lapped around them, caressing them, and the warm night air carried the heady scent of roses—the traditional flower of love. In a blue-lit haze, they were alone, and Banner wanted to stop time.

She could feel the feverish heat of his body and her own; they were pressed so tightly together she could even feel his heart thudding against her. The hardness of his body lent weakness to her own, and his taut tension was hers. When he lifted his head finally, she had no strength even to open her eyes, and her breath was suspended somewhere far away, out of reach.

"Look at me," he whispered roughly.

She forced leaden eyelids to raise, gazing up at a handsome face that was tense and gray eyes that were dark and compelling. Aching from head to foot, she was conscious of nothing but her need for him.

"I want you," he said huskily, his head lowering once again and lips feathering down her throat as Banner instinctively let her head fall back. "You know that."

"Yes." Mindless, she twined her fingers among the silky strands of his thick hair.

"And you want me." It wasn't a question.

But she answered. "Yes," she whispered.

His warm lips traced the swell of her breast as his fingers unerringly found the flimsy string ties of her bikini top. The tiny black triangles fell away and floated aimlessly to one side, unnoticed by either of them. Rory groaned softly. "God, you're so beautiful," he muttered hoarsely. "So tiny and beautiful..."

His hands cupped achingly sensitive flesh, thumbs teasing erotically until her body cried out in a sweet, stinging agony, coming vibrantly alive beneath his touch. Warm lips touched and held, and heat exploded in the depths of her belly and spread like wildfire through every nerve of her body. She arched against him, her hips pressed into his in a primal seeking of possession, a moan shivering from deep in her throat.

Abruptly, Rory caught her in a fierce embrace. Her breasts were pressed against his chest, her face buried in the curve of his neck. He held her with a strength just this side of savagery, and there was a trace of that wildness in the reluctant words that seemed torn rawly from his throat.

"There's still...your Tara," he said thickly.

Banner stiffened, sudden coldness washing her mind and body with sanity. Her Tara, her Tara, which he wanted...

She pulled away and turned her back to him, finding her floating bikini top with one blind, seeking hand. Fumbling to tie the strings at her neck, she choked out, "Why did you—why did you have to—"

"Remind us both?" His voice was rough, hoarse, but the hands that found the remaining two strings and tied them at her back were gentle.

"Yes." Head bowed, she stared unseeingly at

the blue-tinted water, unable to face him because she was afraid of what she'd see in his eyes.

He reached out, pulling her gently back against him, one arm around her waist and the other lying warmly, heavily, across her breasts. "Because I want you to trust me not to hurt you," he said softly, fiercely.

Banner said nothing.

His cheek rested against her hair, and she felt his chest rise and fall against her back as he sighed. "I think we're both a little drunk tonight, milady. Drunk on moonlight and roses...and desire. The easiest thing to do would be to follow our instincts. But your Tara...I think that has to be resolved first—don't you?"

Banner closed her eyes, wishing desperately that he hadn't had to remind them both. She wanted to believe she'd feel no differently about him once the Hall was his, but she knew herself too well for that. A part of her realized and accepted that she would have cut off an arm for him; but losing the Hall would be cutting out her heart.

"Yes," she said tonelessly. "Yes, that has to be resolved."

His arms tightened. "I won't hurt you, Banner. You have to believe that."

Not trusting her voice, she remained silent.

He sighed again. "Tell me what to do, milady. Should I walk away from the Hall and open up the field for another buyer?"

"No," she whispered.

"And if I buy it?"

"I know you'll buy it." She thought of the ghostly soldiers he'd seen, and wondered vaguely if she should tell him she had known, from that moment, he would buy the Hall and live here.

"If I do..." His voice was low and oddly hesitant. "You and Jake could stay here."

"No." She swallowed hard. "No, we couldn't do that."

"Not even if you were my wife?" he asked very quietly.

Banner found that she wasn't breathing. Her heart was pounding violently, and for one single, dizzy moment, she closed her eyes and suspended reality. But she couldn't suspend it forever. In a voice she held even by main force, she said, "That—that wouldn't happen."

"I love you."

Just that, simple and calm. She wanted to cry, but couldn't. And she realized with a peculiar certainty that it would never again be as easy for her to cry as it had been before this moment. Her throat was tight and dry, and she stared straight ahead, silent and blind.

"You'll never be sure, will you?" he mused in that same calm tone. "You'll always wonder if I love you because of the Hall or in spite of it. Or even if I really love you at all. You'll never be sure."

Hearing the words, she knew how certain they both were of the truth of those words. She would always wonder. And neither of them would be able to bear that.

Their beginning was also their ending.

"It's late," she said flatly. "And we have a long day ahead of us."

Silently, he freed her from his gentle embrace. But his hand found hers as they moved through the water and up the steps. He released her hand only long enough for her to don the caftan and for him to shrug into his own terry robe, then his fingers twined with hers once again as they left the pool enclosure and headed back through the garden to the house.

"I'll do my best to convince you, you know," he said conversationally as they neared the veranda. "Rhett might have been worn out by his chase, but I've got more staying power. If it takes me years, I'll teach you to trust my love for you, milady."

Banner knew that her fingers were clinging to his, just as she was clinging to the last instant of this moonlit night when impossibilities had seemed almost within reach. She wanted to tell him that. But an ending was no place for such things.

Just outside the French doors, Rory stopped and turned her to face him, his hands firm on her shoulders. "You think it's over, don't you? You think I'll buy this place, and that you'll leave it—and me—behind. But you're wrong, Banner. We've both got rebel blood; we both know how to fight."

He bent his head suddenly, capturing her lips, kissing her hungrily and possessively. His hands slid down to her hips and drew her against him, making her all too aware that his calm voice had belied a desire that had not ebbed in the least. And that throbbing desire rekindled the hot ache in her own body.

She kissed him back helplessly, unable to deny how his touch affected her. There was still moonlight spilling over them, and she was still clinging to precious moments.

Rory framed her face in gentle hands as he raised his head, his breathing rough and quick. "Fair warning, milady," he said tautly. "The last gentlemanly warning you'll get from me. From this point on, I don't intend to fight fair...because I'm fighting for my life."

"You have one weapon I can't fight," she

admitted unsteadily, honest because she didn't know how not to be.

"And I'll use that weapon," he promised. His lips toyed with hers for a brief, tantalizing moment. "This weapon. And any other I can find. But I won't hold the Hall out as a lure. We both know you'll come to me only because of me, and not for what I can give you. And you will come to me, Banner."

The soft vow held a conviction that stole what little breath she had left, but Banner tried to resist his certainty. "No. You were right. I'd never be sure. I'd always wonder."

"You'll come to me."

She found that her hands were holding his wrists, but she was unable even to try to push his hands away from her. "No."

"Yes."

"Don't do this to me," she pleaded huskily. "It'll make it so much worse when—when I have to leave."

"Leave the Hall? Or leave me?"

"Both," she whispered.

"Do you love me, Banner?"

"You're not—"

"Fighting fair? I warned you." His voice was fierce. "Do you love me?"

"No."

He tilted her face up and covered her lips with his, his tongue probing, possessing. His hands slid downward, exploring her thinly-clad, awakened body with insistent demand. "Do you love me?" he muttered against her lips.

"No—"

Demand shifted insidiously and became supplication, entreaty. His very body wooed hers, his lips pleaded with an aching hunger. Gentle hands caressed with tender care, sensitive and adoring. He held her as if she were a fragile, precious thing.

And Banner's shaky defenses collapsed.

"Do you love me?" he asked, pleading, his voice raw.

"Yes," she cried brokenly. "Damn you—yes!"

He went very still, his lips only a breath away

from hers, his face too shadowy for her to read. "Say it," he whispered.

"I love you...." She felt that she was bleeding inside, something vital torn from her by a will greater than her own. She almost hated him then, because he had forced her to see what would have been less painful if ignored. It would always be there now, a part of the beginning that had been so promising and of the ending there would be no avoiding. She almost hated him. "I love you."

Rory held her close, no demand and no plea in his embrace now, but rather an odd, soothing protectiveness, as if he knew what he had done to her. "I needed to hear that," he said, and breathed softly into her hair.

"It doesn't change anything," she managed unsteadily, the unfulfilled need aching in her.

"Doesn't it?"

"Nothing's changed."

"I love you, Banner."

She wished she could cry. She wished she could hate him. "Rory—"

"I love you."

Defeated, she whispered, "And I love you."

Rory drew back far enough to gaze down at her. After a moment, he kissed her very gently. His eyes were glowing silver, reflecting moonlight—or something else. "You'd better go up to bed, milady. We have a long day ahead of us."

"You—?"

"I think I'll sit out here for a while." He opened the door for her, touching her cheek in a final tender gesture. "Good night."

Silently, Banner went into the house.

Rory closed the door behind her, then turned and crossed the veranda to one of the comfortable chairs. He sat down and gazed for a moment at his shaking hands. Then, grimly, he told himself aloud, "Much more of this and you'll be a gibbering idiot."

He sighed heavily, wishing that he could get drunk. It would, he decided, be a dandy time to get drunk. He hadn't been prepared for his own loss of patience, hadn't been prepared to tell Banner how he felt about her. Somehow, it had just happened. He didn't regret its happening, but he was worried that he might have played his hand wrongly.

Had he driven her away by pushing?

Restless, his body punishing him for his forbearance, he shifted in his chair. His gaze tracked absently across the veranda, then sharpened as he made out a shadowy form among the darkness of climbing ivy near the corner. He started to call out a demanding query, but then a cord of memory twanged in his mind.

Though indistinct, the form was definitely that of a man dressed in the clothing of another century, and moonlight gleamed hazily off blond hair.

Rory was oddly unsurprised, once the first instinctive shock wore off, to see Banner's "guardian" there. He studied what he could see of the watching presence, wryly noting the broad shoulders that were held stiffly with obvious anger.

"Busybody," he accused.

Only chilly silence greeted this.

"All right," he said quietly. "I know it was cruel. I know I pushed her hard and forced her to see something she wasn't ready to see. But I meant what I said. I won't hurt her."

Utter stillness was a condemnation.

Rory sighed. Then, very softly, speaking to himself as much as to the shadowy watcher, he murmured, "I love her. I know what I did to her by forcing those words out of her. I know it wasn't the right time, either. But she's my lady... and I had to make her see that. I have to keep showing her that, proving it to her. Nothing else matters. She has to believe in my love... because she's going to be mad as hell when she finds out..."

His voice trailing into silence, Rory shook his head bemusedly and stared at the empty corner of the veranda.

Well. He'd imagined it, of course.

SIX

BANNER HAD WONDERED what behavior Rory would revert to after the unexpected night of passion. Would he become the cool, businesslike man? The troubled man so aware of his unenviable place in the loss of her home? Or would he return to the bantering, companionable man in whose presence she'd spent a busy week?

The answer turned out to be all of them—and none of them.

He appeared at the breakfast table the next

morning with a cheerful smile for both her and Jake, no signs of his late night marring the handsome face and bright eyes. He greeted her grandfather with his accustomed courtesy, then came to her, tipped her chin up firmly and kissed her quite thoroughly.

Jake contemplated his glass of orange juice with a detached gaze.

" 'Morning, milady," Rory said huskily against her lips.

Banner found herself unable to say anything at all, and only regained her breath when he'd slid into his own chair. Avoiding any glance at her grandfather or Rory, she stared down at her plate and wondered rather wildly if this was what it felt like to be behind battlements that were being stormed by a very determined general. If this particular general's first gesture was anything to go by, she knew what his strategy was.

Hovering somewhere between amusement, excitement, horror, and despair, she realized that Rory intended to make it quite obvious to anyone who cared to observe them together that he was in love with her. In fact, he was well on his way to convincing all and sundry that they were lovers.

It was a strategy she couldn't fight, because a too-large part of her wanted desperately to steal every touch and kiss she possibly could.

And there was the party to get through.

By midafternoon the pool was filled with guests, the garden was being admired by more guests, and the tantalizing scent of roasting food mingled between the hot, still air and hungry people.

Since Banner was both innately and by habit a good hostess, and since she enjoyed parties, the afternoon was a very pleasant one for her. Her only difficulty was the continued campaign of her very determined general. He remained almost constantly at her side, holding her hand or keeping a possessive arm around her waist. He rapidly developed the habit of kissing a shoulder left bare by her strapless sundress, clearly unembarrassed by the amused, speculative glances of the guests. And he called her "milady."

Banner tried—she really tried—to fight him on a level not too obvious to the guests. She introduced him to people and then attempted to slip away while he was occupied—which didn't work, since he kept her firmly by his side. She pleaded the duties of a hostess in overseeing the caterers, only to have Rory maintain—accurately—that since everything had been so meticulously planned, no overseeing was necessary.

But she couldn't fight her own response to his touch and his kisses, and even when those guests who'd attended the costume ball spread the word about the midnight waltz and what it meant, she found herself unable to make it clear to their audience that the truth was something very different.

Jake was no help at all, since he only looked benign whenever asked about his granddaughter's future plans, and maintained an overly innocent silence. He had stopped matchmaking, but then—he hardly needed to now.

Nearly crazy beneath the barrage of Rory's conspicuous attentions, Banner's one consolation was the fact—which he made no effort to hide—that it was driving him crazy as well.

He didn't refer to that until the sun was going down and they were, for once that day, relatively alone. He'd found a place for them in a secluded corner of the garden where there was a comfortable wooden bench and a small table to hold their loaded plates.

"Alone at last," he murmured, smiling at her.

She ignored that. "You," she said roundly, "are a menace."

"Never say so, milady." He kissed her shoulder.

Needing badly to occupy her hands, Banner picked up a barbecued rib and pointed it at him irritably. "A menace. I've been congratulated by total strangers. Three of your business acquaintances from Charleston told me how glad they were that you'd decided to settle down in the area, and one of Jake's oldest friends said he'd been saving his Georgian silver for me for *years*."

Rory was unperturbed. "Nice of him, to say the least."

Banner glared at him.

He laughed softly, then said in a thoughtful tone, "Emeralds would come closest to matching your eyes, but I think diamonds would look best on your lovely hands. What shape d'you prefer?"

"Stop it, Rory."

"You'd rather have something else?" he asked anxiously.

She dropped the rib back onto her plate and twisted her napkin between her fingers, staring down at her ringless hands. "Stop it."

His fingers warm on her cheek, Rory turned her face gently toward him. For the first time that day, his expression was grave and the gray eyes had gone dark. "If I hadn't already known," he said huskily, "today would have shown me how necessary you are to my future.

It's been the most enjoyable, agonizing day of my life, Banner. I have to touch you, d'you realize that? I have to. Even though I know I won't sleep tonight. Even though I know that every touch makes me want you more and more, until I can't think straight. You do that to me, milady."

Banner was drowning in his eyes, trying desperately to stay afloat. "You—you stopped last night," she reminded him unsteadily.

He kissed her with an aching hunger all the stronger because of his taut restraint. "Because I love you," he whispered. "Because I want you to be very sure of what you're doing. Trust me not to hurt you, Banner. Please trust me."

He kept saying that, she realized confusedly, kept asking for that. But how could he, when he knew what the loss of the Hall would do to her? She could only stare at him mutely.

Rory sighed heavily and sat back, his fingers trailing down her cheek before dropping away reluctantly. He seemed to listen to the music coming faintly from the pool area for a moment, then shook his head as if to rid it of some uneasy thought. "We'd better eat while we've got the chance," he said dryly. "The party isn't over yet."

Silently, Banner picked up her fork.

She had wondered more than once why Rory had wanted this party, but somehow hadn't been able to ask him. Maybe that was because she was certain he wouldn't have answered with the truth. And she could think of no good reason herself, unless he simply wanted some of his friends to see the property he would likely buy; but why such an elaborate presentation?

He had introduced her to a good number of his friends and business associates from Charleston and surrounding areas, but none of them seemed aware that he was interested in Jasmine Hall—only that he cared about Banner. And though she was hardly thinking clearly, she saw that Rory's friends—a mixed group of ages and professions—thought a great deal of him. Each seemed sincerely happy that he'd apparently found the woman he wanted, and there was more than one teasing reference as to how happy his mother was going to be.

It wasn't until much later that evening, when the majority of guests were laughingly preparing to climb into hay-filled wagons for the hayride, that Banner finally asked a nervous question.

She gestured toward a man getting into the third wagon along the row—a lawyer acquaintance of Rory's from Charleston—and said, "He wasn't serious, was he? About calling your mother to tell her what her son's up to?"

"If he does, he'll be disappointed," Rory said cheerfully. "She already knows."

"What?"

Laughing, he grasped her tiny waist and lifted her into the first wagon before climbing in himself. "I said, 'She already knows.' " He made himself comfortable in the sweet-smelling hay, then calmly pulled her onto his lap. "I called her days ago."

Under the noisy cover of people getting into the wagons, she hissed wrathfully, "Damn you,

Rory Stewart. You're putting me in an impossible situation."

He pulled her even closer, the bright moonlight showing her his rueful smile. "I told Mother," he murmured, "that I'd finally met the right woman and that she was hell-bent on refusing me. Mother was very amused; she can't wait to meet you. As a matter of fact, she'd have been here today, except that she had to be in Atlanta to help my sister with her new baby."

"I didn't know you had a sister," Banner said, distracted in spite of herself.

"Mmmm. And a niece and a brand-new nephew. They all want to meet you."

Banner stirred uneasily, then realized abruptly that certain actions weren't very wise when sitting on a man's lap. His arms tightened around her almost convulsively, and the gray eyes glittered with a sudden flash of fierce emotion.

He groaned softly. "If we were alone..."

But they weren't. Yet, when the wagons moved out, they discovered a curious intimacy between them. In the fragrant hay, the other guests seemed to have found the same thing, for couples sat close together, whispering softly, as if they were in a world of their own. The moonlight was bright, and the creak of the wagons and soft thuds of the teams' hooves lulled everyone into just relaxing and enjoying the night.

Conscious of his jean-clad thighs beneath her own, Banner found it difficult to relax—particularly since the wagon wheels apparently had minds of their own when it came to finding ruts in the dirt road. Each jolt caused the passengers to sway inevitably, and made Banner tautly conscious of his building desire.

"This isn't very smart," she breathed, but made no objection when he drew her head down to rest on his shoulder.

"I know. God...I know." He didn't release her, however. One of his hands dropped to the middle of her thigh, rubbing slowly and rhythmically, while the other gently massaged the nape of her neck.

Banner's eyelids lowered slowly, with the languor of desire rather than sleepiness. She felt a shudder go through him and her breath quickened, matching his. Dazed, she tried to remember that she had known him just a week, tried to recall her belief that love would be a gradual thing. But it was no good. She loved him, and since he had forced her to admit that—to him and to herself—she could no longer ignore it.

She wondered why her trust was clearly so important to him, wondered why he was so determined that the situation with the Hall be resolved before they became—inevitably—lovers. Banner didn't want to wait, because she knew very well that once the Hall was his, she would have to walk away from him. Her pride would allow nothing else.

And she didn't believe that was what he wanted; she might not be able to trust in his love, but his desire for her was very real, and very strong. No, he wanted them to become lovers as badly as she did. What was it he'd said? That she would come to him?

Banner tried to think it through, tried to figure out why he was waiting, what he was waiting *for,* but she couldn't. She was too aware of his body and his touch and his desire, and too aware of her own shivering need.

For the first time in her life, she deliberately and consciously pushed the Hall out of her mind.

By the time the wagons had wound their way back to the house, the other occupants had sung half a dozen songs that neither Banner nor Rory heard, and midnight was an hour past. Most of the guests were staying overnight, and as they clambered down from the wagons it became apparent that few were ready to turn in yet; the pool still held a strong appeal.

While the others brushed away clinging strands of hay and started back toward the pool, Banner silently and reluctantly left Rory's lap. She didn't speak until he'd jumped lightly to the ground and reached up to swing her down; then she spoke quickly and huskily, mistrusting her nerve.

"Are you going to turn in, or—"

His hands at her waist, Rory stared down at

her for a long, silent moment. He seemed to catch his breath as he gazed on her upturned, moonlit face and wide, consciously inviting eyes, then a rough sigh escaped him.

"No. No—I think I'll join the others at the pool. How about you?"

She heard the reluctance in his hoarse voice, but that didn't soften the blow of rejection. Stepping back until he dropped his hands, she said in a carefully even tone, "I think I'll call it a night. See you in the morning."

"Good night, milady."

She turned away and headed quickly for the house, and if she had heard his soft and heartfelt *"Damn!"* behind her, she might have slept more easily. But she didn't hear, and she hardly slept at all.

Banner skipped breakfast the next morning, although she did come downstairs in time to see off what looked like the last of the guests. Rory was there as well, cheerful as usual, but his façade dropped abruptly when he caught her hand and she tried to pull it away.

"What's wrong?" he asked quietly as they stood in the open doorway and watched cars heading down the long driveway.

"Nothing." Since he hadn't released her hand, she could hardly turn and walk away, as she wanted to.

"You didn't come down for breakfast."

"I slept in."

"Did you?" He turned her suddenly to face him. "There are shadows under your eyes, milady. You didn't sleep at all."

"Gloating?" she asked evenly.

His free hand came up to cradle the side of her neck. "Is that what you think?" he asked seriously.

Incurably honest, she gave her head a tiny shake. "No."

"Good," he said flatly, "because sending you off to bed alone last night was the hardest thing I've ever had to do in my life."

"Nobility," she offered shakily, even while she marveled at the fact that neither of them seemed able to pretend with the other.

He laughed on a sighing breath. "No. Hardly that. I want more than one night from you, Banner. More than one night *with* you." A faint light of self-mockery showed in his eyes. "I swam in that damn pool all night; I haven't been to bed at all."

"It doesn't show," she murmured, gazing up at him and seeing no signs of too many hours without sleep.

Rory shrugged. "It doesn't with me. Some things don't. Maybe that's why a certain lady could...misunderstand."

"What else have I...misunderstood?" she wanted to know, her voice soft.

"My priorities," he said simply. "You come first with me, Banner. Don't ever lose sight of that."

Before she could respond, Conner had approached with his silent tread and apologetically interrupted them.

"Excuse me, Miss Banner, Mr. Stewart. Mr. Clairmont wonders if the two of you would join him in the library."

As they turned toward that room, Rory said suddenly, "That reminds me—whatever happened to that book you were going to let me read?"

Shifting her mind to unimportant things, Banner shrugged. "I looked for it the other day, but couldn't find it. Maybe Jake knows where it is."

"Well, it's not important," he said, unconsciously echoing her thoughts. "I just wondered." He halted before opening the library door and carried her hand to his lips. "Trust me," he added in an entirely different voice.

Banner went into the library as he released her hand and opened the door, wondering why she could never answer a simple yes to that plea. It wasn't as if she didn't want to. . . .

Two men rose from their chairs as she and Rory entered the room, her grandfather and another man who had introduced himself to her yesterday as a friend of Jake's. His name was David Moore, and he was a silver-haired, sharp-eyed man of about Jake's age.

"Banner," her grandfather began, "you and Rory have met David, haven't you?"

"Yesterday," Banner agreed, watching Moore and Rory shake hands; the older man seemed amused, and there was a tiny frown on Rory's face. Before she could think about that, Jake was waving them to chairs and going on briskly.

"David was asking me about something, lass, but I think it's up to you to answer."

She looked enquiringly at the other man, who seemed a bit uncomfortable. "What is it, Mr. Moore?"

"First of all, Miss Clairmont, I have to apologize for invading your privacy."

"In what way?" she asked, surprised.

"Well, yesterday during the party, I was wandering around the grounds and happened to stumble onto your little cottage in the woods." His eyes gleamed with sudden wry laughter. "Being human, and curious, I looked in the window."

"I see." Banner smiled at him. "I could hardly not forgive human curiosity, Mr. Moore."

"Thank you. And what I was asking Jake was whether or not he thought you'd allow me inside that cottage. I would very much like to take a closer look at the painting I saw yesterday."

Banner was surprised, and it was her turn to be uncomfortable. "You'd be disappointed, I'm afraid. I'm just a hobbyist."

"Still," he said persuasively. "I'd like to see it."

"And so would I," Jake put in, giving Banner a very old-fashioned look. "From what David tells me, lass, you've been hiding your light under a bushel."

Banner's eyes sought support from Rory, who merely said in a dry voice, "I've told you what I think of your work."

"Which is?" Jake asked curiously.

"It's damned good."

"May I see that portrait?" Moore asked again.

She shrugged helplessly. "Well, I suppose there's no reason why not. But please don't expect too much—whatever Rory says."

But when the four of them stood in Banner's

cottage studio contemplating her portrait of the
blond gentleman, Moore didn't seem in the least
disappointed. Chin in hand, he stared consideringly at the painting for a long moment.

"Did Rory sit for you?" he asked absently.

Something about the question bothered
Banner, but she couldn't pin down exactly what
it was. "No. It's ridiculous, I know, but I painted
that purely from my imagination."

He grunted softly, but made no other response
to that. He merely said, "I'd like to look at more
of your work."

Puzzled and a bit uneasy, Banner assented.
Rory helped her to take canvases from the stacks
around the room. They leaned the paintings
against the walls or furniture, so that they could
be seen. It was Jake who spoke first.

"I'll be damned," he said, oddly hushed.
"Why didn't you show these to me, Banner?"

"After all . . . it's just a hobby, Jake. It isn't important." She was increasingly bewildered, because none of the men seemed to agree with
what appeared so obvious to her.

Moore walked around, picking out half a dozen of the canvases, choosing a variety of subjects, and leaning them all around the easel holding the blond man's portrait. Then he stood back and stared at them for endless moments. "Look at the feeling for color and line," he murmured, as if to himself. "And *life*. The detail. And the brushwork is superb."

"Thank you," Banner managed to say, stunned by the curious and sudden muted passion in his voice.

He turned to her then, his sharp eyes alight with what looked like excitement. "You've never had a show, Miss Clairmont, and I'd like to give you one."

"A show?" she said blankly.

"In New York. I have a gallery there."

"But—" To Banner, this enthusiastic offer was more than a shock. She had never even imagined her work displayed for the public to see and judge. Fear washed over her.

He seemed to see that fear even as she did.

"Miss Clairmont," he said quietly, "you obviously don't realize it, but you have a very great talent. Artworks are more than a hobby to me— they're my life. And I can promise you that you could name your own price for any or all of these paintings."

Banner sat down rather suddenly on the tall stool and stared at him. Then she stared at Jake. Then at Rory. All three nodded encouragingly. "I—I don't know what to say," she murmured finally.

"Say yes," Moore very nearly pleaded. "I'd consider it an honor to show you and your work to the art world."

Only dimly aware that her entire life could be changed for good or ill when the public saw her work, Banner took her courage in both hands and nodded. "It's...my honor, Mr. Moore. And thank you."

Ten minutes later, Banner was still sitting on the stool. Jake and Moore had returned to the house, Moore literally rubbing his hands together in excitement and already planning phone calls to begin making arrangements. Banner and Rory were alone in the cottage, and she was stunned.

"But I've never had any training," she said incredulously. "I learned from books, for heaven's sake!"

"And by painting." Rory stood before her, smiling.

She stared at him, then laughed unsteadily. "I can't believe this. It's like something out of a dream...or a nightmare. Rory, what if they don't like my work? What if they laugh at me?"

"They won't," he promised firmly. "Moore isn't the only one who knows something about art, milady; I know a bit myself. And I'm quite sure that you're going to be a famous lady very shortly."

"I'm afraid," she admitted. "I'm afraid I'll regret this."

He pulled her to her feet, smiling down at her.

"Wouldn't you regret it much more if you didn't take the chance?" he challenged quietly.

"I—yes, I suppose so." She shook her head. "I know I would."

Gravely, Rory said, "In that case, may I buy the future talk of the art world a cup of coffee? I don't think she had any breakfast."

In the new and bewildering excitement of a soon-to-be showing of her work in New York, Banner should have found it easy to think of things other than Rory.

Should have. But didn't.

David Moore was remaining at the Hall for a few days, making his arrangements by phone. From his gallery in Charleston, he'd borrowed a couple of his men to crate her paintings carefully for their shipment to New York. He had asked gravely that he be allowed to give her a second show later on, at the Charleston gallery, so that the South could admire the work of one of its own, and she had assented even while wondering if there would be a second anything after the critics in New York finished with her.

All of this should have been a diversion from Rory and from the way he made her feel simply by entering a room and smiling at her.

But he was never out of her thoughts, and she no longer even tried to fight him—on any level. She became as unembarrassed as he by possessive touches and passionate kisses, uncaring if Jake or Moore or the servants witnessed.

They swam together, rode together, walked together. They talked late into the night about pasts and thoughts and ideas. They listened to music and played Scrabble and chess and poker. Familiarity grew between them, the automatic facades of acquaintances falling away to reveal the bare and vulnerable surfaces willing to trust.

And though desire was never more than a touch or a glance away, laughter helped to smooth the rough edges of passion.

"I really hate to complain again, milady, but I woke up sneezing this morning. That jasmine scent was gone—or I thought it was—for a while, but now it's back."

They were sharing a late breakfast this morning, and Banner sent him a wry look across the table. "Is it?"

"Yes. I asked Conner, and he said the maids didn't use jasmine-scented freshener, or jasmine-scented anything else, for that matter. Maybe I could move to another room."

Banner sighed. "I'm afraid that wouldn't do any good, Rory."

"Why not?"

"Because it isn't the room. It's what...uh, comes into the room."

He stared at her. "I beg your pardon?"

She sneaked a glance up from her orange juice, fighting a smile. "Well, you see, it's Mother."

"Your mother? But she's—"

"Uh-huh."

Rory drained his orange juice with all the air of a man who wished it were something considerably stronger.

Smothering a giggle, Banner said, "Mother always wore jasmine; she loved it. So apparently she's—uh—visiting you."

"Why?"

"You'd have to ask her."

"I don't suppose there's another—logical—explanation for the jasmine scent?"

"You're welcome to come up with one. If you can."

"You're enjoying this!" he accused her.

"Immensely."

He sighed. What's her name?"

"Mother's? Sarah. Why?"

"I just want to be able to ask her politely why she's visiting my room."

"Let me know if she answers."

"I'll do that."

SEVEN

By the middle of Rory's second week at the Hall, Banner's paintings were on their way to New York, and so was David Moore. He had set a tentative date for the showing of barely two weeks away, at which time Jake and Banner would also be in that city.

Banner didn't know what Rory's plans were. They didn't talk about the showing or about the future of the Hall, both tacitly preferring to take each day as it came. And each day was becoming more difficult for them.

It was hard to say whether their honesty made things worse; neither of them pretended or tried to hide their desire. The entire household—led, needless to say, by Jake—entered into a conspiracy to leave them alone together as much as possible, which tried both Rory's patience and Banner's pride considerably.

She had made up her mind that the next move—if, indeed, there was to be one—would come from him. Another rejection on top of her fear about the showing would be more than she could handle, and she knew it. But the restless, sleepless nights were hard. And there was no satisfaction for her in the knowledge that the nights were just as hard on Rory.

Rather than attempt any more postmidnight swims, she began creeping through the silent house and out to her cottage studio, there to work harder than she'd ever done in her life. The portrait of the blond gentleman was finished—though not in time for the New York show, for which she was curiously grateful. It reposed on an easel beside the new work. The painting she worked on now was of Jasmine Hall, a subject she had never before felt qualified to attempt. And after three nights of steady, driven work, it was nearly finished.

She made no mention of the painting to either Rory or her grandfather; the painting had become, for her, a private farewell to the Hall.

And it was that symbol of finality, her own determination to paint what was lost to her, that finally made Banner face a future she'd avoided considering so successfully until then.

It was Thursday, and somewhere near midnight; the painting was finished. It sat on her easel, a glowing representation of a home that had housed generations. And she had, in unconscious whimsy, hinted at those generations long dead. Near the corner of the veranda among the darkness of ivy, she had bent sunlight to her will and had it shape the vague outline of a light-haired man in the dress of a century before. At one upstairs window, a fluttery curtain and vague shadows hinted at a presence. And in the rose garden, which occupied the background on the right of the painting, wisps of a morning mist might have been Rebel soldiers strolling with their brides.

Banner never heard the thud of her palette dropping to the floor. She stared at the painting and the pain of loss throbbed in her. Jasmine Hall...and Rory.

She didn't turn off the lights or close the door behind her; she simply ran for the stables, desperate to get away from her own thoughts. But they followed her relentlessly as she bridled a startled El Cid and grasped his thick mane to swing aboard his bare back, and they followed her as willing Thoroughbred legs ate up the ground in long strides.

Why, *why* couldn't she believe that she could live here with Rory no matter who actually owned the Hall? Why was her awful despair at the thought of losing the Hall mixed with an equally powerful despair at losing Rory?

Did she have to lose them both?

Her mind, ignoring all commands to blank it-self, inexorably examined the situation and her own feelings about it. Pride. Was it simply pride that told her she would have to lose them both? Did it really matter so much to her that another name would be on the deed? If she married Rory, it would be *her* name as well as his; there would never be another Clairmont to inherit the Hall no matter what happened.

And then she realized, slowly, that it *was* her pride. For generations, Clairmonts had main-tained and preserved the Hall. And now she, the last Clairmont daughter, could do nothing—*nothing*—to save it for the family. With a bitter laugh that echoed in the darkness and caused Cid's ears to flick back nervously, she recalled Rory's parallels. Scarlett O'Hara had saved *her* Tara, she remembered self-mockingly. She had killed for her family and her Tara, had ruined her delicate hands and bowed her back working in the *dirt* to save her beloved Tara. She had schemed for it, pinched pennies for it, worked herself and her family relentlessly for survival and for Tara. She had entered a man's world and fought by her own rules. And in the end, she had saved Tara and lost the man she loved.

And what could Banner Clairmont do to save *her* Tara?

She could marry the man who wanted them both. But the empty ache inside of her was an agonizing denial of that option. Yes, that would save the Hall and keep her within it; she would see it flourish beneath Rory's guiding hand, she knew. Family name or no, descendants of Clairmonts would continue on in the home of their ancestors.

But she would never be *sure*.

Never be sure that the Hall had not seeped into Rory's blood more thoroughly than she ever could. Never be sure that he had not wanted the one because it was a part of the other. Never be sure that he loved her more.

And which, she asked herself then, honestly, did she love more? For a moment, a split second, she was torn. Then the pain ebbed, and she knew the answer. Rory. That was why she would leave him. She would leave him, not because her pride wouldn't allow her to live with him in *his* Jasmine Hall, but because she would never be sure just how much he loved her.

She wanted him to have the Hall if she couldn't keep it herself. He would take care of it. She would turn her back on the home that was a part of her and leave. She would turn her back on the man she loved more than her heritage and leave him because she couldn't bear being second in his heart.

"Trust me."

She wished she could.

Rory stared at a shadowy ceiling, unable to sleep and not the least surprised by that. He was still fully dressed and lying on top the covers, having known that he wouldn't sleep. He thought of Banner and of the things they hadn't talked about these last days. The future of the Hall. Her show.

So much depended on that, though Banner

herself hadn't realized it. Would she realize, he wondered, when she found out what prices would be asked for her paintings? Would she realize when she saw—as she inevitably would—that people were willing and eager to pay those prices? She had no conception of the scope of her talent, no idea at all just how gifted she really was.

Would she realize that her talent would allow her to keep the Hall?

Jake had realized, Rory knew. The old man was, of course, delighted, though clearly cautious; he would wait until the show before he would abandon plans to sell his plantation.

Rory would have told Banner himself, but he knew she wouldn't believe him. She would have to attend the show and find out for herself.

But the waiting was so hard....

And how would she react when his own involvement became apparent? If it did. If not, he'd tell her himself. Would she trust him enough to see why he'd done what he had? Or would her stubborn pride blind her to his true motives? It was that definite possibility more than anything else that had shored up Rory's patience these last days. He wanted her to be sure that he wanted her more than the Hall.

Of course, once she could be sure that the Hall would be hers, she could still suspect him of wanting them both. But no matter what he did, that possibility existed—unless he walked away, and then she still could lose her home. Rory would have willingly given up the Hall for Banner, but not at the cost of hurting her. She needed the Hall and he needed her.

He wondered, then, which she needed more—him or the plantation. He wondered if she had asked herself that. He didn't know the answer. He knew that he loved Banner, and wanted her no matter what the price. And he knew that if she agreed to marry him, it would be because she loved him. Nothing else mattered.

Rory sighed, then sat up abruptly as he sneezed. He realized then that the scent of jasmine had grown heavy in the room, so heavy that he was forced to breathe through his mouth or be racked by sneezes. Frowning, he gazed around the darkened room. His eyes followed the shaft of moonlight as it cut a bright path from window to door, then he caught his breath, absently swallowing another sneeze.

The door was open.

He distinctly remembered closing it, and knew from experience that it had a good, strong catch.

"Sarah?" he ventured uncertainly. Instantly, he sensed movement, agitated movement, and the scent of jasmine grew even stronger.

Startled, Rory swung his legs over the side of the bed. Clearly, his visitor wanted something of him, but he didn't know what it was. "I'm not a mind reader," he told the visually-empty room, then almost laughed when he distinctly sensed irritation and impatience. "I hate to say it, but give me a sign." He told himself he'd laugh about this in the morning.

The curtains at one window fluttered.

A bit hesitantly, he left his bed and moved to the window. Since the house was centrally air-conditioned, the sash was down, but Rory didn't let himself think about that; he just parted the curtains and gazed out and down on an empty moonlit garden. After a moment, he turned back to face the room.

"There's nothing there," he complained.

More impatience, and then the door swung slowly, until it was almost closed, before swinging open again.

"You want me to go somewhere?"

Instant approval.

Rory obediently left his room. In the hall, he hardly knew which way to go, but then he saw what he immediately took to be his guide at the top of the stairs. The blond man. Shadowy and indistinct, he was nonetheless *there,* and Rory started for him, unable to ignore his own curiosity.

His blond guide led him down the stairs and out into the garden, always staying just far enough ahead that Rory had to strain to see him. He wondered absently why he could see this ghost but only feel Sarah, then wondered irritably why he was wondering.

He was obviously dreaming the whole damned thing.

Just as he realized they were heading for Banner's studio, he saw that lights were shining within and the door was open. He forgot his guide and hurried forward, uneasy because two ghosts had roused him in the middle of the night and both had clearly been upset.

He stepped into a cottage that seemed curiously bare, with only blank canvases leaning against the walls. Two completed paintings—the blond man and one Rory hadn't seen—reposed side by side on twin easels. The new painting was of Jasmine Hall, and he stood staring at it, feeling the raw emotion that had gone into the work.

Before he could do more than absorb the subject and the sadness it aroused, he heard the sound of thudding hooves, and made it back outside just in time to see El Cid's black form sharply etched in the moonlight as he galloped away from the stables and across the field, a small, familiar figure hunched on his back.

Without thinking, Rory ran for the stables.

Banner heard a shout behind her, heard the sound of pursuing hooves. For an instant she nearly reined in her mount. But then she leaned forward even more, her fingers tangled in Cid's thick mane and her knees pressed tightly to his sides. She didn't know why she was courting danger with this wild ride across fields and over fences, but she urged her horse on. El Cid, with the blood of wind-racing Arab ancestors in his aristocratic veins, lengthened his stride until he seemed to barely skim the ground, and took wing over every jump.

It was, in a sense, a release of tensions and cares, a flirting with danger, that helped to satisfy her body's craving for another kind of release. Or so it seemed to Banner. She felt free and stingingly alive, breathless with the excitement of her dangerous night ride.

The pounding hooves behind her pursued, but she had no fear of their catching her. El Cid and Shadow were half-brothers, both sired by a racing Thoroughbred, but the Cid was just a touch faster, and he had the advantage of a lighter rider. And the racing fever was in his blood, just as it was in his rider's; born to fight any restraints or restrictions, the Cid was running wild.

Banner didn't realize she had lost control over her mount until she automatically tried to turn him away from a looming obstacle she never would have attempted even during daylight: a wicked four-rail fence bordering a sheer drop of several feet, at the bottom of which was the wide stream that ran through the plantation. Heart in her throat, sobered at last by sure disaster for herself and her beloved horse, Banner tried desperately to turn her racing mount away from that impossible jump. But the Cid had the bit between his teeth and was hell-bent on the impossible, refusing to heed even the commands of the only person he had ever obeyed.

Realizing the futility of trying to stop the horse, Banner swiftly considered and discarded the option of jumping off him. She wasn't overly worried about her ability to land safely; she'd taken too many tumbles in her life not to know how to land with the least risk to herself. What did worry her was the Cid. He was going to take that jump with her or without her; at least with her on his back, she might be able to keep him balanced enough to give him that vital extra chance of making it.

With only seconds to prepare, she hastily loosened the reins and grasped his mane as firmly as possible, leaning all her weight forward and using all the strength in her knees to hold her seat firm. Then she urged him on aloud, knowing that he would need every ounce of speed and determination to jump high enough and far enough to land on the far bank.

Like any incredible feat, it was over almost before it began. El Cid cleared the fence with a foot to spare, his powerful hind legs launching him with driving determination. Banner saw the flash of water passing far beneath them, felt the horse's forward velocity slow and his body stretch catlike in midair as he reached for the opposite bank of the stream. They were dropping, flying, falling.

Incredibly, impossibly, the Cid's front hooves touched the bank and dug in. He stumbled as his speed caused him to lurch forward, but Banner's quick hands on the reins held his head up until his hind legs were under him and he was balanced again. It was the last thing she was able to do before her own slipping balance and the horse's second lurch forward unseated her.

Deliberately disobeying the first rule of riding, she dropped the reins, then let herself fall. Like an expert tumbler, she rolled as she touched the ground, cushioned by the thick meadow grass, unhurt. And she sat up instantly, her heart in her throat for a second time as she remembered the pounding hooves only strides behind.

Shadow was little more than his name as he hurtled over the fence; the moonlight that had etched the Cid's black form only turned the gray horse indistinct and eerily unreal. But however dissimilar they were in color, the blood they shared, told that night. Rory's mount took wing just as Banner's had, stretching in midair and then clawing for that vital bank. And he made it.

Rory was slowing the gray and sliding off in the same motion, leaving the horse to go wherever it would as he hurried to Banner's side. He dropped to his knees, filled with anxiety, his hands finding her shoulders.

"Are you all right?" he demanded roughly.

"Yes. Yes. I'm fine." Her voice was shaking, and she wasn't surprised by that; the rest of her was shaking too.

He eased back on his heels, but didn't release her. "Just an easy middle-of-the-night ride, huh?" he asked wryly.

"Seemed like the thing to do," she managed to say. "At the time."

Rory glanced over at the jump they'd both just taken, then went very still. Obviously, he'd had no time to realize what had happened. In an extremely careful voice, he said, "Is *that* what we just jumped?"

"Uh-huh."

He turned his gaze back to her, gray eyes glittering in the moonlight. Then he shook her. Hard.

"What *possessed* you," he gritted out, furious, "to risk a jump like that? Bareback, the dead of night, after a three-mile race at a gallop—you could have been killed!"

This last roar caused Banner to wince, but she wasn't at all resentful of his rage. She could hear fear for her as well as anger in his voice, and wondered amusedly when he'd realize that he had taken the same jump and the same risks—even more so, since he hadn't been familiar with them, as she had.

A bit breathlessly, she managed to answer, "Better ask what possessed the Cid; he was running wild."

"That brute's going to get you killed!"

"It was the first time he ever disobeyed me—"

"Once is all it takes, Banner."

She sighed. "It was my own fault. I encouraged him to run flat-out."

"Why?" Rory demanded wrathfully. "And why didn't you answer when I called out to you?"

Banner gave herself a moment to think as she glanced toward the horses, noting that they were grazing calmly only a few yards away. "I don't know," she said finally, looking back at him. "I guess...I went a little crazy, like the Cid. I wanted to—to run."

"From what?" His voice was suddenly quiet.

"Do you have to ask?"

"I asked you to trust me," he reminded.

"I know you did."

He was silent for a moment, then said, "I saw the painting."

Banner said nothing.

His hands tightened on her shoulders. "It's beautiful—perfect. But it isn't good-bye, Banner."

For the first time, she pushed his hands away from her. Getting to her feet, she walked over to her horse and patted his damp neck before un-buckling and removing his bridle. "Grass instead of your stable tonight, boy," she murmured. "You've earned it." To Rory she said only, "We ran in a circle. Ironic, huh?"

"Banner—"

"We can leave them here in the meadow for the night; Scottie'll see them in the morning, since the stables are just over there. I'm . . . going back to the cottage for a while." She didn't wait for him, but tossed the bridle over her shoulder and struck out across the meadow toward the woods.

He caught up with her quickly, carrying his own bridle. "Banner, we have to talk."

She kept walking, silently passing through the gate he opened, then following the path leading toward the cottage. She said nothing until lighted windows came into view, then spoke softly without looking at him.

"What's there to talk about, Rory? That's what I faced tonight, what I was trying to run from."

He waited until they were inside the cottage, watched while she hung both bridles on pegs by the closed door, before he said, "That's it, then? There's nothing else to say?"

Banner felt tension steal through her at his flat, strained tone. Not looking at him, she went over to stand before the easels. "Nothing."

"Can't you trust me not to hurt you?" Rory wanted to tell her that she'd be able to keep her home, but since art was something no one could be certain of—public acceptance being a fickle beast—he wasn't about to get her hopes up. And his inability to ease her mind tortured him. "Banner, I love you. Believe *that*."

Banner turned slowly to face him. Vaguely, she was aware that the night's wild, dangerous ride had left tendrils of recklessness in her, but she didn't care right then. "It doesn't change anything. I told you that." A part of her, an ancient, feline part of her, watched intently, waiting. "There's no use pretending anymore, Rory."

"I haven't been pretending," he gritted out.

"I have." She stared at him. "Just like in your

favorite book; I keep pretending I'll think about it tomorrow."

He stepped toward her, face taut. "Banner—"

"But tomorrow's here." She gestured jerkily over her shoulder at the image of Jasmine Hall behind her. "Tomorrow's that painting."

One long stride brought him to her, and his hands went to her waist, hauling her against him. "I won't let you throw us away," he muttered against her lips. Then he was kissing her hungrily, all the pent-up frustration of two weeks driving him.

Banner didn't even bother to hide her exultation. Her arms lifted to slide round his neck and she rose on her toes to fit herself more fully against him; recklessness held her as firmly as he did, recklessness and a desire she wasn't about to fight—or let him fight. She wanted no reminders about her Tara. She didn't want to wait for some vaguely promised tomorrow when everything would be all right. She wanted him, and saw no reason to pretend about that.

He tore his mouth from hers. "Banner—"

"I love you," she whispered, pulling his head back down, kissing him fiercely.

A groan rumbled from deep in his chest as Rory's mouth slanted across hers, deepening the kiss until it was a literal act of possession. Smoldering desire flared to new life, fed by her fiery response, until there was no possibility of restraint.

He lifted her into his arms, carrying her into the bedroom, where a shaft of light from the studio illuminated the bed and left all else in shadow. Setting her gently on her feet beside the bed, he framed her face in his hands for a long moment, gazing down at her. Raggedly, he accused, "Dammit, you planned this."

"A gentleman wouldn't notice that," she murmured huskily, her own hands lifting to cope with the buttons of his shirt.

Rory's laugh was half groan, but his fingers were no less eager than hers when they trailed down the V neckline of her summer blouse. "You're no lady, milady," he teased, his lips feathering along her jawline and down to her throat.

"Right now, I don't want to be a lady," she breathed.

Shirt and blouse dropped to the floor, shoes and jeans were kicked aside, unimportant and forgotten. Underthings were smoothed away by eager, impatient hands, until they stood with no barriers between them.

She looked at him in wonder, sudden heat blooming somewhere deep inside of her and spreading rapidly all through her body. He was so beautiful it made her throat ache, and the emotion in his eyes as he gazed at her own body made her feel more beautiful than she knew herself to be.

He caught his breath harshly, drawing her fully against him for a tantalizing moment before bending to strip back the covers of the bed, then lifting her onto it.

Banner stretched out her arms to him as he came down on the bed with her, her breathing quick and shallow, her body trembling. Her fingers tangled in his hair when his lips lowered to hers, and the touch of him fueled her hunger until she was dizzy with it.

Rory held her restless body still as he lay half over her. He kissed her closed eyes, her brow, her cheeks, pressed long, drugging kisses to her trembling lips. Though his own body was taut and fever-hot, he seemed determined to torment them both. Slowly, lazily, as if they had all the time in the world, he learned her body. Hands molded and shaped quivering flesh, lips explored with tender, sensitive hunger.

Desire coiled tighter and tighter within Banner, becoming a consuming need that ran molten fire through her veins. A hollow agony grew in her middle, expanded, filled her whole being. Heat suffused her skin, and her hands gripped his shoulders with white-knuckled tension. His seeking touch probed erotically and tore a moan from the depths of her throat as she moved with restless impatience.

"Rory..."

"God, I need you," he groaned hoarsely,

moving over her, gazing down on her with hot, liquid eyes. He kissed her deeply, tenderly, then raised his head to look at her taut, seeking face. "And I love you," he whispered, moving with gentle care.

Banner caught her breath, surprise and wonder widening her eyes. Her arms tightened around his neck in instinctive possessiveness. A part of her was suddenly unleashed and out of control, a wild, primal cave-woman exultant in the certainty of being loved by her man. She caught him within her fiercely, trapping them both in a fiery union that threatened to consume them.

Smooth rhythm quickened, desperately hurried by need. Breathing caught and jerked convulsively as feverish bodies drove themselves on a reckless flight toward satisfaction. Hearts pounded frantically within their living cages, and two voices were barely human as they cried out words of love....

Banner refused to let him leave her, murmuring a soft plea before he could do more than begin to shift his weight.

"I'm too heavy," he whispered against her throat.

"No." Languidly, her fingers explored the sharply defined muscles of his damp back and shoulders. She watched the light from the main room glimmer on his bronze flesh, and not even the faintest tinge of regret disturbed her contentment.

Rory sighed, his breath warm on her. "You're so tiny, milady. I'm afraid I'll hurt you."

"No." She touched his cheek as he lifted his head, smiling into his arresting gray eyes. "No, you won't hurt me."

He knew what she was saying, and he had to swallow before he could manage a light tone. "If I'd known what'd change your mind, I wouldn't have been so damned patient all this time."

She was still smiling, a curiously mysterious, feline smile. "I changed my mind before we ever got back here to the studio," she murmured.

"What *did* make you change?"

"Seeing you take that jump." Her smile faded, replaced by remembered anxiety. "I could have lost you, you know. I've seen horses go down on easier jumps. When Shadow landed safely I... I just knew I had to take the chance."

"You trust me," he said, his voice and expression full of wonder.

She pulled his head down to kiss him lovingly. "Of course I trust you, idiot," she murmured against his lips.

Rory lifted his head suddenly, a martial light growing in his eyes. "Wait a minute, now. If you felt that way before we came back here..."

"Mmmm?" Banner decided that she most definitely liked the taste of his skin.

"Then what the hell was the meaning of all that malarkey?"

"Malarkey?" She was mildly offended. "That was no malarkey. I meant every single word I said."

Frowning, Rory concentrated for a moment, then realized that everything she'd said could have been taken in a way other than he'd taken it. "Well, the *way* you said it was malarkey," he accused sternly.

"Oh, no, it wasn't." She brushed a lock of thick blond hair away from his brow and smiled gently. "And you half-guessed that yourself. It was a very careful, if spur-of-the-moment, plan."

"You little witch!" he said blankly.

Banner took that as a compliment. "Well, you were so busy being noble all over the place that I had to do something. And it worked nicely, don't you think?"

"It worked." He stared down at her with a mock frown. "Although I'm not too sure I care for being manipulated."

"Better get used to it," she warned serenely. "Southern ladies are famous—or should I say infamous?—for it. Remember your favorite heroine?"

"What've I let myself in for?"

She let her nails move slowly across his back and murmured, "I really couldn't say."

Rory shuddered, and his voice had hoarsened when he spoke. "I'm not so sure myself. But I think—*I know*—I'm going to enjoy every minute of it." And his mouth hungrily found her smiling lips.

EIGHT

"ONE OF US," Rory murmured sometime later, "should go and turn off that light."

"You're elected."

They were lying close together, with only a sheet covering them, and the light from the main room bathed the bed in brightness.

"I," he responded politely, "couldn't move if the place were on fire."

She giggled. "Likewise, I'm sure."

"I don't suppose it'd hurt anything to leave it on?"

"I doubt it." She was silent for a moment, then asked curiously, "What brought you out here tonight?"

"I . . . couldn't sleep."

Hearing the faint note of discomfort in his voice, Banner raised herself on her elbow and stared at him. "Rory?"

He avoided her eyes for a moment, then sighed ruefully. "Well, hell. They're your ghosts, after all."

She blinked. "Ghosts brought you out here?"

"Literally." He managed to keep his voice light as he told her about why he'd left his room in the middle of the night, finishing with, "When I saw the painting, then heard a horse and went out to see you tearing across the field—well, I didn't stop to think." He touched her cheek gently. "I suppose they . . . thought you needed me."

"They were right. I did." She gazed at him gravely. "When I saw what I'd painted, I thought—it's over . . . and I ran."

"And now?" he asked softly.

"You tell me."

He frowned just a little. "Could you...live here with me? No matter who owned the Hall?"

"Yes." Then, honestly, she added, "But I think I'd always feel that I let the family down somehow. Oh, it isn't logical, I know. But I can't help believing that I should be able to save the Hall myself. I can't help feeling that, Rory. I want to be able to say it doesn't matter, but I can't."

Quietly, he replied, "You said you trusted me not to hurt you."

"And I meant that."

"But I'll hurt you if I take the Hall."

Banner tried to work it through in her own mind, then realized abruptly why that was impossible. Because the question was no longer a matter of *thinking*...it was a matter of *feeling*. Every instinct she possessed told her that though Rory now held the power to hurt her in many ways, taking the Hall from her was no longer one of them.

She didn't know why. Perhaps because she

believed he loved the Hall *almost* as much as he loved her. And that was really all that mattered.

"No, you won't." Banner smiled at him. "Not if we live here together. Not if we work together to preserve the Hall. And not as long as you know that you're more important to me than it is."

Rory caught his breath, then pulled her head down and kissed her fiercely. "I didn't hope for that," he murmured against her lips. "The Hall's in your blood."

"So are you," she whispered achingly. "So are you."

The light in the main room went out just then, leaving only the moon's glow to brighten the bedroom.

"Power failure?" Rory ventured cautiously.

Banner rested her cheek against his chest, smiling. "Somehow...I don't think so."

"Well," he said after a moment, philosophically, "at least the ghosts of Jasmine Hall are helpful spirits."

Giggling, Banner relaxed completely in his arms and allowed sleep to float her away.

———

She woke to the appetizing aroma of bacon and coffee, and lay there with her eyes closed for a moment, frowning. She couldn't, she thought uneasily, be smelling bacon if she were in the cottage, because there was no kitchen.

Had she dreamed last night?

Then warm hands surrounded her face, and she looked up into smiling gray eyes. "Good morning, milady," he murmured, kissing her gently.

" 'Morning." She was immensely relieved, but confused as she took a good look at him. "You're dressed."

"Only because I had to go get breakfast," he explained, bending down as he sat on the edge of the bed, and retrieving a huge, heavily loaded tray from the floor.

Banner sat up with a laugh, tucking the sheet underneath her arms. "You got enough to feed an army. I know you didn't fix all this yourself!"

"I sweet-talked the cook," he said disarmingly.

"And then met Jake in the small dining room on my way out."

"Oh, great. I'll never hear the end of it."

"Nonsense. He was a perfect gentleman about the situation."

"Oh?"

"Yes. He said he was going to go find his shotgun."

She chuckled in spite of herself. "To which you replied—?"

"I pleaded moonlight and a Southern hussy as extenuating circumstances."

"I'm sure he appreciated that."

"Completely. He said blood would tell. He meant yours, I gather."

Banner sipped her coffee demurely. "Well, to hear him tell it, my grandmother seduced him one moonlit night."

"And people think Southern ladies are *ladies!*" Rory snorted.

"We are ladies." She leaned forward to kiss him, allowing her fingers to trail across his cheek

as she sat back. "Until we're forced by...
circumstances...to be something else."

He caught her fingers to his lips. "Did I happen to mention how much I loved your 'something else,' milady?" he asked huskily.

"No," she replied firmly, "you didn't."

"Well, I loved it. There's just something about chasing a lady in a three-mile circle on horseback in the dead of night, taking a jump that should have killed the both of us, then being deviously seduced, that's quite...enjoyable." He answered her giggles with a mock frown. "I'm serious!"

Banner reclaimed her hand and picked up a piece of bacon, still laughing softly. "If you say so. It just sounded so comical."

Abruptly serious, he said, "That jump wasn't comical. I admire your horsemanship tremendously, but I'd be very grateful if you wouldn't attempt another jump like that."

"I'll have a talk with the Cid," she said agreeably. "Just between you and me, I was praying for wings last night. I've never taken a jump like that in my life, and don't intend to do so again."

Rory leaned back on an elbow, drinking his coffee and smiling at her. "Good. I don't want to lose you now."

"You took the jump too," she reminded him.

He winced. "But I didn't know what I was doing. All I saw was the fence and you going for it like a bat. I didn't know there was a sheer drop and a creek on the other side."

"And if you had known?"

"I would have prayed for wings too."

They spent the day together. Jake maintained a discreet absence, and all the Hall servants, from Conner to the gardeners, seemed to have entered into a conspiracy to leave the lovers to themselves.

They swam in the pool for a while that morning, competing amicably over their diving.

"What was *that?*"

"A swan dive, milady."

"Really?"

"Personal best."

"I can do better."

"Prove it."

After her graceful dive, Rory admitted she was better, but qualified the statement by saying he'd been paying too much attention to her form to pay attention to her *form*. To which Banner pulled on a ludicrously expressive "how like a man" grimace, and challenged him to better her backward flip.

For lunch they packed a picnic basket and strolled off across the fields, finding a shady spot beneath a towering oak and spreading a blanket there. In the warm midday stillness, both food and sleep held strong appeal—but so did other things.

"You're very handy, you know," she observed at one point.

"Talented—that's me."

"I mean it literally. As in 'all hands.' "

"Mmmm. D'you know that you have utterly fantastic—"

"Oh, good, chocolate cake for dessert."

"And you're blushing. That's a lost art."

"Well, I just found it."

"Suits you, too."

"Have some cake."

"I'd rather have you."

"Right here in a field?" she asked politely.

"On a blanket. We'll have a pagan ritual—how does that sound?"

"Creative."

"And?"

"And I think I'd better wrap the cake back up..."

Banner had believed that the past two weeks had made her accustomed to his touch, but she discovered the difference between the touch of a lover and the touch of a man who wanted to be a lover.

There was a new tenderness in him, and their familiarity with each other seemed only to sharpen his fascination with her—and for her.

Each touch lingered and each glance seemed to deepen, heavy with promise. And light words only added to the depth of feelings, rather than masked them.

"D'you know my toes curl up when you smile at me?"

"I'll make a note of that."

"And that my heart turns flips like a landed fish?"

"Interesting."

"And that I can't breathe?"

"Rory, maybe you'd better see a doctor."

"There's no cure for what I've got, milady."

"They're making *tremendous* advances in medical science."

"If they can't cure the common cold, they sure as hell can't cure lovesickness."

"Maybe they could give you shots to lessen the effects."

"I think I'll just suffer bravely through it."

"My hero."

"Your hero is hungry."

"You should have eaten the cake."

"That was hours ago. No wonder I'm starving."

"Well, it isn't time for dinner yet."

"Let's raid the kitchen."

"If you love me, you won't irritate the cook; she's the sixth one this year."

"No man hath greater love than mine."

"Good."

"I'll *sneak* into the kitchen...."

They spent their nights in the cottage, warm, magical nights of love and ever-deepening desire. Although Rory was usually up first, he awoke late one morning and found Banner awake, dressed only in his button-up shirt, and leaning against the brass footrail of the bed with a sketch pad on her knees.

"What're you doing?" he asked sleepily.

She didn't reply for a moment, the charcoal pencil in her fingers flying over the page. Then she looked up with a smile, tucking the pencil behind an ear and turning the pad so that he could see it. "Sketching you."

In a few delicate lines and with soft shading, she'd captured him as he lay on his stomach, face half-buried in the pillow. The sheet rode low over his hips, and a shaft of sunlight through the window cast highlights and shadows over his tanned body and sleeping, unaware face.

Rory stared at the sketch for a long moment, coming fully awake. He was first startled by the completeness of his image, by the fact that she'd been able to depict him so totally with only spare lines and shading. Then the similarity between himself and that imaginary man out in the studio struck him more strongly than ever before.

"That's me?" he ventured uncertainly, seeing more character in the sketch than he thought his own face held.

"It's you." Then, softly, she added, "Asleep. With all your defenses down."

He looked at her. "That's why you sketched me?"

"D'you mind?"

He reflected for a moment before answering. "No. I've seen you asleep and vulnerable, after all. But do I look so different awake?"

Banner laid the sketch pad aside and stretched out on her side, facing him. "If you want to see how you look awake," she advised, "go out into the studio and look at the Southern gent. It's you, Rory. I don't know why it started out looking so much like you, but I finished it with you in mind."

Since he'd studied the painting often during the past couple of days, Rory was quite familiar with it. "Then you've paid me quite a compliment," he said wryly.

"Not at all. I just painted what I see every time I look at you."

Rory drew her slowly toward him. "I wish," he whispered huskily, "I could paint you the way I see you. But I've no talent in that area, milady. And even if I had talent, I don't think I could paint my Banner." His fingers found the charcoal pencil and tossed it toward the sketch pad as he rolled gently to pull her on top of him. "How could I paint a soft voice and laughter, to say nothing of impossibly green eyes? How could I paint a touch that sends me to heaven and a warm and beloved presence I need so badly at my side? How could I paint quick intelligence and humor—and a temper I've been warned about but never seen?"

"I think," she murmured just before his lips touched hers, "you've more talent than you know...."

Quite some time later, she asked curiously, "Who warned you about my temper?"

"Jake, of course."

"Treacherous snake. What'd he say?"

"That you could flay the hide off a man wearing a suit of armor while standing twenty paces away and without raising your voice above a soft murmur."

"He exaggerates."

"He called that an understatement."

"He would."

"I, of course, defended you."

"Oh, yes?"

"Certainly. I told him that there was no way my lady would be so undignified as to do something like that."

"Thank you."

"She'd *smile* while flaying the hide off an armored man at twenty paces without raising her voice above a soft murmur."

"How would you know? I've never gotten mad at you."

"I know that, and it's like waiting for the other shoe to drop."

"Why do I hear the sound of a guilty conscience in those words?"

"I can't imagine."

"Rory?"

"Milady?"

"Is there something you want to tell me?"

"Not at the moment, no."

"You sound like a little boy caught with his hand in the cookie jar."

"I feel like I'm sitting on a keg of dynamite—and I'm not about to hand you a match."

"You're making me nervous."

"Then you know how I feel."

"I think we'd both feel better if that other shoe dropped."

"Do you? I, on the other hand, would prefer that it never touched the ground."

"Rory."

"Trust me."

"How can I, when you think it'll make me mad?"

"I don't think it'll make you mad. I'm reasonably *sure* it'll make you mad."

"This is getting worse by the minute."

"What I'm doing, you see, is appealing to your intelligence."

"How so?"

"Well, when I finally do confess my horrible crime, you'll remind yourself that you're going to surprise me by not getting mad."

"Sure about that?"

"Can't blame a man for trying."

" 'Horrible crime,' huh?"

"Figure of speech."

"Why am I playing guessing games with you instead of hitting you over the head with a rolling pin and demanding an answer?" she wondered thoughtfully.

"Because you're a lady," he answered, wounded.

"That's never stopped me before."

"You make a practice of hitting men over the head?"

"No, but my flaying ability has been honed to a fine art."

"I thought you said Jake exaggerated."

"I lied."

"Deceitful wench."

"The pot's *definitely* scorning the kettle. Are you going to confess?"

"I think I'll let you calm down first."

"Who's not calm? I'm calm."

"There are danger signals in your lovely green eyes, milady."

"Your imagination. Confess."

"I think I just heard Jake calling us—"

"Confess!"

"When the sun goes down. There's more room to hide in the dark."

With a very thoughtful—and unthreatening—expression, Banner slid from the bed and began dressing, fully aware of Rory watching her in enjoyment. "You aren't going to confess, then?" she asked musingly, fastening her shorts, then standing with hands on hips as she gazed down at the man on the bed.

"I'd rather put it off as long as possible," he admitted.

Frowning slightly, she bent to gather his clothes from the floor, then straightened. "Sure?" Her tone was that of a woman who wants to be very certain of her facts.

Rory began to get uneasy. "I'm sure." Stalling for time, he reached for his watch on the nightstand and peered at it. "Hey—breakfast should be ready. Want to hand me my clothes?"

Her frown dissolving and a gentle smile

growing, Banner slowly backed toward the door. "Not really," she said sweetly.

He sat up, alarmed. "Banner? Where're you going?"

"Breakfast," she reminded softly.

Rory glanced down at the tangle of sheets that was his only covering, wincing as he remembered the gauntlet of servants he'd have to run from the cottage to his bedroom—where spare clothing was located. Then he looked at her with foreboding. "You wouldn't."

She lifted a gently inquisitive eyebrow as she stood in the doorway.

"You would," he realized hollowly.

"Confess?" she invited in a gentle tone.

"I won't submit to blackmail!" he declared firmly.

"Fine." She turned away. "See you at breakfast." Then she threw one parting bit of advice over her shoulder. "Better come get it while it's hot." And dashed from the cottage with Rory's curses tinting the morning air blue behind her.

It couldn't have worked out better for her;

Jake had decided to have breakfast on the veranda, and was sitting at the table with his morning paper when she hurried up the steps.

Handing the bundle of clothing to Conner, standing ever-ready behind Jake's chair, she said cheerfully, "Have these taken to Mr. Stewart's room, would you, please, Conner?"

"Yes, Miss Banner." With no flicker of curiosity on his impassive face, the butler vanished into the house.

Jake frowned at her as she slid into her chair. "Where's Rory?" he asked.

"Oh, he'll be along." Banner sipped her orange juice and smiled slowly. "If he can rig a toga for himself, that is."

The green eyes so like her own began to gleam as Jake rather ostentatiously folded his paper and laid it aside. "A toga, is it? And why would he do that, lass?"

She meditatively chewed a bit of bacon. "Well, he could use a fig leaf, I suppose, if he could find one. But a toga would...cover more territory."

Her grandfather was obviously biting the inside of his cheek to keep his mirth at bay. "I see. What've you've done, girl?" he demanded with a fine show of irascibility.

"I stole his clothes," she explained solemnly.

Jake coughed rather hard, then bent a fierce stare on her. "Why?"

"He made me mad."

"I warned him." Jake shook his head sadly. "The name isn't Irish, but the blood is. I did warn him."

"So he told me."

"Just to give him a fighting chance, you understand," her grandfather explained blandly.

"Oh, of course."

The blue-tinted curses began to reach them faintly.

Jake listened for a moment, then said approvingly, "Hasn't repeated himself once."

"He's half Southern, you know."

"That'd explain it," Jake agreed gravely.

"Ummm. I thought about having Conner line everybody up to see the show."

Jake thought about that for a moment before giving his opinion. "No, that'd be a bit excessive, lass."

"That's what I decided. No need to embarrass the poor man, after all."

The curses were growing louder.

"Certainly not," Jake affirmed solemnly.

Bare feet slapped the steps as Rory climbed them with a methodical tread. Banner and Jake gazed at him, both faces calm and detached, taking in the brilliant green sheet wrapping his lean form in a toga that demanded both the wearer's hands to remain in place.

" 'Morning, Rory," Jake ventured carefully.

Rory came to a halt on the veranda, fulminating gray eyes shifting from one to the other of them as if seeking to fix the blame for his predicament on someone other than himself.

"Coffee, Rory?" Banner asked politely.

He took a deep breath and grabbed at a slipping bit of green linen. Then he glared at Jake. "Your granddaughter," he said roundly, "is a vixen! A she-devil without scruples, manners, morals, or an ounce of fair play in her devious little heart!"

"That's very good," Jake noted consideringly.

"I object to the no-manners bit," Banner said, elbow on the table and chin in hand as she stared thoughtfully at Rory. "I'll concede the rest, but I'm very well-mannered."

"You're a little witch!"

"If I were a witch," she told him sedately, "I wouldn't have left you the sheet."

"Where're my clothes?" he demanded.

"In your room, of course."

Jake shook his head mournfully at his guest. "I did warn you, my boy. Never get a Clairmont mad at you. *Especially* a Clairmont woman. Like to see my battle scars?"

Momentarily distracted, Rory stared at him. "Your wife wasn't a Clairmont, was she?"

"Not until I married her." Jake smiled reminiscently. "But once she came here to live . . . And then there was my mother. And Sarah, Banner's mother. Banner herself, of course. I've got scars from all of 'em, my boy. I wasn't kidding about

the need for armor—for all the good it does."
He stared at Rory. "Your breakfast is getting
cold."

Rory absently clutched a slipping fold of the
sheet, his gaze going to Banner. "Are you going
to steal my clothes every time you get mad at
me?" he wanted to know, somewhere between
incredulity and bemusement.

She sipped her coffee. "Oh, no. I'll think of
something else next time."

Jake grinned suddenly. "My Elizabeth came
up with some dandy ways of relieving her temper," he said fondly. "Once, at a hotel, she threw
all my clothes out a window while I was taking a
shower. And another time, she hired two men to
impersonate the police and arrest me in the middle of a dinner party."

Rory stared at him. "Wouldn't it have been
simpler to just have a good knockdown, drag-
out fight?" he asked wryly.

Jake gave him a pitying look. "You'd better
learn to understand Clairmont women better
than that, my boy, if you mean to hitch your

wagon to one. They're *ladies,* you see. Never raise their voices or lose their smiles when they're mad. They just...get even."

Rory made a sound somewhere between a groan and a sigh. "Wonderful. And the men who marry Clairmont women?"

Lifting his coffee cup in a slightly mocking toast, Jake said, "They roll with the punches, my boy. Rather like the Lady and the Tiger. You've heard of that? Well, a man married to a Clairmont woman—if he knows his woman—would be damned sure there'd be a tiger behind the door she told him to open. So he'd pick up a big stick and open the door."

Fighting his way through the analogy, Rory managed to ask, "Why wouldn't he just open the other door?"

"Well, he could do that, of course," Jake agreed dryly. "But his woman would make sure there was a second trip into that puzzle. And this time—there'd be a tiger behind *each* door."

After a moment, Rory looked at Banner and

said severely, "If you ever tell me to open a door, I'm picking up a *gun!*"

"Better make it a big one," she advised serenely.

Rory sighed.

"Coffee?" Jake invited cheerfully.

"Hell. Why not." Tucking his makeshift toga more securely about his lean form, Rory slid into his chair and reached for his coffee cup. And he didn't even wince when Conner came back onto the veranda and subjected him to a detached gaze.

NINE

"You're not going to confess, are you, Rory?"

"Are you kidding? After seeing what you did just because I wouldn't confess, I dread what you'll do when I tell you what I actually did."

"That's a tangled explanation. Besides, don't you realize that my imagination's conjuring terrible horrors?"

"I'm not an ax murderer."

"I wonder."

"Or a felon of any kind, for that matter."

"Then *tell me*."

He kissed her. "I have other things on my mind right now."

"Like how you looked in that sheet?" she asked, unmoved.

He winced. "My darling love, can we discuss this later?"

"How much later?"

"Um...after your show? No need to get you upset before then, is there?"

Banner looked at him suspiciously, then relented at his hangdog expression. "I suppose not. But you're going to tell me...right?"

"Of course," he assured her instantly.

"My mother told me never to trust a Yankee. I should have listened."

"I'm only half Yankee."

"That's the half I don't trust."

Rory sighed. "Why don't we go for a ride?"

They were standing alone on the veranda, both dressed in jeans and casual shirts, and Banner had just returned from replacing the cottage's lost sheet.

"All right."

"Meet you at the stables," he said. "I have to make a quick call." When she looked at him again suspiciously, he said dryly, "I've been here longer than I planned, you know; I need to re-arrange a couple of appointments."

Only partly reassured, Banner headed for the stables. But halfway there she remembered she'd left her riding crop on a table in the foyer, and doubled back to the house.

She couldn't find the crop in the foyer and, muttering to herself, crossed to the partially open library door and went in, wondering if she'd left the whip in this room the day before. But she instantly forgot about that.

He had his back to her, but his end of the conversation reached her. Loud and clear.

"No, David; you won't reimburse me for the cost of the party! I threw the thing for fun as much as to get you down here without arousing Banner's suspicion. Having you see her work was the main objective, but not the only one. Are you set up for the show yet? Good. How about that list I sent with you? They're all going to attend? Great. Well, they're all collectors of Southern artists; you ought to make some dandy sales. Yeah. Maybe it'll convince her she's really good. Sure. Okay. See you then."

Banner closed the door soundlessly by leaning back against it, and stared across the room at his back while he cradled the receiver. She had thought that loving Rory and trusting him had set her pride behind her; she discovered in that instant how wrong that thought had been.

Generations of proud, stubborn Southern blood ran hot through her veins and floated redly across her eyes.

He had *arranged* it. He'd thrown his weight around deviously in order to get a New York gallery owner down here to *just happen* to stumble across her studio and see one of her paintings. So *that* was the "horrible crime" he'd been reluctant to confess—and no wonder!

In a flash she knew why he'd done it, and a part of her was instantly warmed by the love that had driven him deviously to help her to save her home herself. She loved him too much, by this time, to suspect that he was merely making sure he got both her and the Hall; their nights and days together had convinced her that she was on top of Rory's list of priorities, just as he was most important to her. So she didn't suspect his motives.

But she was furious at the way he'd gone about helping her—assuming, at any rate, that the show *would* help her to save the Hall. She was furious, and calm descended over her in an impenetrable veil of serenity, behind which her mind worked methodically.

Rory turned away from the phone and halted abruptly, staring toward the door, just scant feet away. She leaned against the solid wood panel calmly, arms folded beneath her breasts and her lovely face wearing a gently inquiring expression. She appeared about as unthreatening, he thought, as a woman could possibly be.

And the memory of his toga-clad dash across the garden made him wince inwardly.

"Uh...how long have you been there?" he asked carefully.

"Long enough."

Her voice, he reflected, was as quiet and musical as always. No temper flashed in her green eyes, and her lips were curved slightly in a faint smile. He began to get nervous.

"Banner, I can explain."

"Really?" she asked politely.

"It isn't what you think. All I did was to ask David to come down here and look at your work. The show was his idea, I promise you."

"You know him quite well, then."

"Yes." Rory admitted reluctantly. "He's a friend of my mother's."

Banner nodded as though a strong suspicion had been confirmed. "I should have known. When he asked if you'd sat for the blond gent's portrait, he used your first name—as if he'd used it for years."

"Your memory's too good," Rory complained.

"Oh, my memory's excellent."

He winced openly now. "I should have told you. I should have asked you if I could invite David down here. But I was afraid to get your hopes up, so—"

"*My* hopes?" she queried lightly.

"About the likely results of your show. You'll be able to keep your Tara, milady. If the show goes the way David and I think it will, you'll have enough capital to turn the Hall into a paying proposition in some way."

"Your loss," she commiserated gently.

Rory knew very well that the last thing he needed to do was to lose his own calm; he also knew, after this morning, that her smiling calm was a danger signal. So he took a deep breath and tried to make his own motivation very clear to her.

"Banner, I love you. And I couldn't stand the thought of seeing your home taken away from you—even by me. It was an underhanded thing to do, I admit, without telling you, but I wasn't sure enough of my own knowledge of art to take the chance of disappointing you."

"I see."

He stared at her warily. "And understand?"

"Of course I understand, Rory." She smiled. "I love you too."

After a moment, he said guardedly, "You loved me this morning—but you still stole my clothes."

"Temporary aberration," she said dismissively, and casually waved her hand.

"From what Jake said, that's a common thing with Clairmont women," Rory reminded her, still uneasy.

"Oh, he was just talking through his hat. Testing the steel, so to speak, of his prospective grandson-in-law. Always assuming that's what you're going to be, of course."

Rory frowned at her. "You aren't mad enough at me to refuse to marry me over this, are you?"

"Did I say I was mad?" she asked innocently.

"You didn't have to. And answer the question!"

"Actually," she said in a contemplative tone, "I haven't heard a real, honest proposal. I've heard a lot of promises, mind you. You even said I'd come to you—which, in a manner of speaking, I did. But I'll be damned, Rory Stewart, if I'll do your proposing for you."

He blinked. Then he purposefully crossed the space between them and took both her hands in his. Lifting them in turn to his lips, he said huskily, "Will you marry me, milady? Marry me and share my life? Marry me and let me help you to preserve this lovely home?"

Banner freed her hands so that she could slide her arms around his waist. Smiling tenderly, eyes glowing, she said, "I've just been waiting for you to ask, love."

"Is that yes?" he murmured, his breath warm on her lips.

"Very much yes."

He kissed her gently, relief flowing through him. Then a sudden realization tempered that relief. "You haven't said you forgive me," he managed to say, his body rather bent on things other than conversation.

"No, I haven't, have I?" she whispered.

Rory drew back and stared down at her. "Banner?"

She was busy tracing the curve of his lips with one thoughtful finger. "Yes, love?"

"What've you got up your sleeve?" he asked warily.

She sounded wounded when she said, "What a nasty, suspicious mind you have."

"Banner."

"Darling, do I seem mad to you?"

The endearment forced words to lodge in his throat for a moment, but then with determination he forced them out. "No, and that's what worries me." He stared into green eyes that glowed with a newly seductive and vastly distracting light. Fighting distraction, he forced out more words. "Jake said that Clairmont ladies get even when they're mad. Just what've you planned in that devious mind of yours?"

"But, Rory, what you did was for me and the Hall, wasn't it?"

"Yes—"

"Then why should I have anything to get even *for?*"

"I schemed behind your back, remember?"

"Maybe you'd better not keep reminding me."

He looked toward the ceiling for help. "Now it's really like waiting for the other shoe to drop."

She stepped back, smiling at him. "I thought we were going riding."

Rory gave up...for the moment. "Instead," he challenged, still not entirely convinced she'd agreed to marry him, "why don't we drive into Charleston and pick out a ring?"

"All the trappings, huh?" she teased softly.

"You betcha. I'm going to marry you, milady—even if the other shoe *doesn't* drop."

She grinned at him suddenly as she turned to open the door. "I'll drop it on our honeymoon!"

"You wouldn't dare!" he yelped, remembering too late that daring her was entirely the wrong thing to do. He followed her hastily from the library and caught her hand as they headed for the front door, adding anxiously, "Would you?"

"Thinking of the 'Sorry, love, I've got a headache' ploy?" She stopped in the foyer and smiled up at him, but both her smile and her eyes were very serious. "That's one promise I'll make you right now, Rory. I'll never use sex as a weapon— or a reward. That would be cheating the both of us, and twisting what we feel for each other. I'll never do that."

"Neither will I," he promised softly, his fingers twining with hers. "Now let's go pick out that ring, milady."

They were halfway to Charleston before he remembered she still had reason to get even— *and* that her heritage was crammed with ancestral ladies with a creative talent for that sort of thing—but by then he lacked the nerve to open the subject again.

They made a day of it in Charleston, returning in time for dinner. And Jake was delighted to be shown the flawless oval diamond solitaire adorning his granddaughter's left hand.

"We'll have an engagement party," he decided happily.

"After the show, Jake," Banner said in a firm tone. "I can only handle one crisis at a time."

"Thanks a lot," Rory told her.

"You're welcome."

After their meal, Banner left Jake and Rory alone with brandy in the library, explaining that she had things to take care of with the staff, since the family would be leaving for New York in a few days. And it wasn't until then that Rory sought advice of a man experienced in Clairmont women.

He explained his deception even though he was reasonably sure Jake had guessed most of it already, then finished with, "Do I expect her to try to get even, or not?"

Amused, Jake said, "She won't *try*, my boy. She'll either get even or she won't."

"You think she will?"

"She's a Clairmont," Jake murmured.

"Oh, great."

"You can't say you weren't warned, Rory."

"I know, I know. But what do I expect this time?"

Jake sipped his brandy thoughtfully. "My boy, I have sixty-some-odd years of experience with Clairmont women. I've seen them mildly insulted, faintly irritated, slightly angry, and mad as hell. I've seen them relieve those feelings within seconds and I've seen 'em wait months to get even. I've seen revenge that was quick, just, fitting the crime, damned embarrassing, and hysterically funny. I've never seen cruel or hurtful revenge."

"And so?"

"And so . . . your guess is as good as mine, my boy. Your guess is as good as mine."

A little blankly, Rory said, "I've hitched my wagon to a loaded gun."

Jake nodded slowly. "But it'll never hurt you, Rory. It'll just make one hell of a bang."

Rory rose to get more brandy. "I'm already bracing myself for the noise," he confessed.

"That's always wise," the older man agreed. "Because you've only got one sure thing to hold on to."

"Which is?"

Jake's sharp green eyes were unfocused, far away in memory, and he was smiling softly. "Your Clairmont woman. They're unlike any other, Rory. They sprang from stock that brought charm and grace to a raw new land. They speak softly and gently, hiding their steel. They understand without being told that they're as strong as the strongest man, and they fight when they have to."

Rory smiled just a little. "Scarlett and her Tara," he murmured.

Looking up, Jake returned the smile. "Most people come away from that book thinking there were two kinds of Southern ladies," he said wryly. "Melanie, the gentle, fragile flower, seemingly weak but somehow strong. And Scarlett, determined, strong-willed, selfish, passionate.

Clairmont women are both of those—and neither. Unlike Melanie, a Clairmont woman would never look to another for strength. And unlike Scarlett, she'd never lose the man she loved because she didn't understand him.

"That's something you can always be sure of, Rory. You'll never be able to say your wife doesn't understand you...because she always will."

Rory thought about that. There was something both exciting and strangely unsettling about being known that well. As much as he loved Banner, he didn't feel that he completely understood her. Yet, at the same time, he understood her better than any woman he'd ever known. And what he *didn't* understand about her intrigued him.

Like her temper. He was, as he'd said, already braced for a sudden bang. He was wary enough to feel the need to peer round each corner before he turned it. But he was also aware of bemused fascination. He hadn't needed Jake to tell him that a life with Banner would be well worth the—he hoped—infrequent bangs of her temper. If nothing else, it would certainly keep him on his toes!

He left Jake alone in the library and went in search of his wife-to-be, finding her upstairs, talking to one of the maids. She turned to him as the maid went on down the hall, sliding her arms up around his neck and smiling.

"Jake offer you any advice?"

"D'you think I'd ask him for any?" he managed after a startled moment.

"I know you did, love," she said serenely.

"I have *definitely* hitched my wagon to a loaded gun."

"Guns are no danger." She smiled. "If you know how to handle them."

He sighed. "I think I'd better learn that...real quick."

Her fingers moved to his shoulders. "You're tense," she noted, frowning slightly.

"D'you blame me?" he retorted.

She didn't respond to that, but took his hand

and began leading him toward her bedroom. "I know just the thing to relax you."

Rory followed a bit warily, saying nothing until she was closing the door behind them in her bedroom. "Just what'd you have in mind?"

"Strip," she ordered cheerfully.

He blinked. "The last time you got my clothes off, milady, you stole them."

"I never repeat myself," she advised.

"Still, I'm not going to take my clothes off unless I put them under the pillow!"

She laughed as she turned toward the connecting bathroom. "If it'll make you feel better."

Cautious, but curious in spite of himself, Rory removed his clothing and placed it over a chair near the bed. When she tossed him a towel from the bathroom and instructed that he lie across the bed on his stomach, he began to realize what she had in mind. But he waited until she was sitting on the edge of the bed, opening a bottle of oil, before he commented.

"Massage? Where'd you learn that?"

"I read a book. Now, close your eyes and relax."

Given the inescapable fact that he had only to be near her to feel fiery desire, it seemed incredible that the touch of her hands could possibly put him to sleep.

But there was magic in her fingers, her strong, slender artist's fingers. Magic that loosened taut muscles and seemingly sapped all energy. She was silent as her hands moved over his back, kneading muscles gently and firmly, gliding smoothly over oiled flesh. He felt boneless within minutes, and slipped into a deep, utterly relaxed sleep before he even realized it.

When he woke, the lamplit room was still and quiet. And he was alone in the bed and covered with a sheet. He focused on the clock on the nightstand, surprised to find that it was nearly midnight. His clothes were still lying over the chair, and his robe lay across the foot of the bed. He sat up and reached for the robe, wondering where Banner was, then made a startled discovery as he realized his entire body was glowing with oil and feeling wonderfully relaxed from the massage.

Staring blankly at the wall, he muttered, "I slept through that?"

"You certainly did," Banner said in amusement, closing the hall door behind her as she came into the room. "But then—that was what I wanted you to do."

Pained, he demanded, "How could you let me sleep through one of the high points of my life, milady?"

"I'll wake you up next time," she apologized gravely.

He pulled her down beside him, then frowned. "There's a smudge of green paint on your nose. Have you been working while I slept off the effects of your wicked fingers?"

She rubbed the smudge away, only saying in a vague tone, "Fancy that."

"Banner—" He was uneasy, and wasn't quite sure why.

"I love you," she said solemnly, gazing into his eyes.

"I love you, but—"

"Do you realize no man's ever slept in my bed before?"

Distracted, he said in mock horror, "What . . . never?"

"Never. You'll be the first to spend the night here."

"Ummm." He gazed at her, saying thoughtfully, "My father always said never to be the first at anything—to wait and see if anybody died from it."

She slipped her arms up around his neck, smiling. "Next stop heaven?"

"I'm game," he murmured, just before his lips found hers.

Rory found himself distracted quite a bit during the next few days. And he always seemed to be distracted just at the moment when he was wondering where Banner kept disappearing to. She would get him involved in something, whether it was talking to Jake or watching a young Thoroughbred being trained by Scottie, and then vanish. Anywhere from an hour to several hours later, he'd find her occupied with some innocuous chore, such as cutting flowers or discussing the evening's menu with the cook.

It was the *in-between* that bothered him.

But his future wife was maddeningly elusive. She never gave him a chance to ask what was going on, always distracting him with a seductive smile or an innocent remark—both of which were virtually guaranteed to put his mind on things other than questions.

"Jake, she's planning something!"

"I'd say the planning stage was past, lad. She's probably—um, executing the plan right now."

"D'you know what she's doing?"

"I'm just guessing, lad."

Rory was guessing as well, and his guesses led him to her cottage studio—where he found a cosy little cottage bare of any artist's paraphernalia. Only two completed paintings reposed placidly on easels. Her worktable, paints, brushes, blank canvases—all gone.

He ran her to earth in the rose garden, where she *hadn't* been only ten minutes before, and was determined not to be distracted this time.

"Banner, where's all your equipment?"

She looked up from her kneeling position before a splendid Crimson Glory and smiled at him. "Oh, I've moved it."

Dropping down to sit cross-legged beside her, he frowned. "Why? And where?"

She was weeding industriously. "Why—because I wanted to. Where—that's none of your business, darling."

Rory was unoffended, but uneasy. "You... just wanted someplace private to work?" he guessed.

"Something like that. You don't mind, do you, darling?"

"I'm not quite sure," he said slowly. "You aren't—uh, busy getting even, are you, milady?"

"I'm weeding, Rory."

"You know what I mean."

"You worry too much," she told him firmly.

"I think I haven't been worrying enough."

Banner changed the subject abruptly. "You know, you never did tell me what you bribed Conner with to get him to accept that Creole cook during your party."

Absently, he replied, "What? Oh, that. I just told him I needed his cooperation and help in my courtship of you, that's all. That butlerly exterior hides the soul of a romantic."

She laughed softly. "So that's why he keeps glancing at my ring with a look of triumph. I did wonder."

Rory blinked. "You're a devious wench! I wasn't going to tell you about that."

"Caught you with your guard down, didn't I?"

"And distracted me again too. Banner—"

"I haven't asked you if you're going to New York. You are going with us, aren't you?"

He sighed, abandoning his fruitless probing. "I certainly don't want to miss your first show. I'm coming even if you tell me not to."

"Why would I do that?"

"Revenge?" he suggested dryly.

"Rory, I'm surprised at you!"

"Are you?" he asked even more dryly.

She giggled suddenly and got to her feet. "Not really," she confessed. "I rather thought you'd been worried about that."

"Wouldn't care to set my mind at rest, I suppose?"

"Not just yet," she responded gently, offering him a hand up.

Rory took the hand and rose to his feet, sighing again. "You're a devious, unscrupulous, conniving little witch, Miss Clairmont, and I can't think why I love you so much."

"Amazing, isn't it?"

Having lost her for several hours on the day before they were to leave for New York, Rory was on the veranda when he heard her rather battered VW pull into the drive and up near the side of the house. He got to his feet, but had barely crossed to the steps when she came running lightly up them.

Before he could ask, she said cheerfully, "Just

a few last-minute things I had to take care of in Charleston. Have you packed for the trip?"

"I even packed a suit of armor," he said, slipping his arms around her as they stood together on the top step.

"Ah. Suitable for being flayed in, I assume?"

He winced. "That's a painful word."

She kissed his chin. "Darling, I love your body just the way it is—unmarked." Then added wickedly, "Trust me."

"It's just that the other shoe's taking a damned long time to drop," he explained.

"It should make a satisfying thud, then, don't you think?"

Rory groaned. "Milady, I'm going to do my damnedest never to get you mad again!"

TEN

THE TRIP TO New York was uneventful. They'd reserved a suite in a hotel fairly near the gallery, and spent a couple of hours settling in before taking a taxi to see how David Moore had set up for the show, which was scheduled to open the following day.

Banner surprised Rory by not appearing the least bit nervous; she was cheerful when David met them at the door, and didn't seem at all disturbed by the coming ordeal of public and critical scrutiny of her work.

It made Rory very nervous.

David conducted them on a tour of his gallery, explaining how and why he'd placed each of Banner's paintings as he had. Then he took the three of them—Banner, Rory, and Jake—out to dinner. He was unashamedly excited about the show, especially since everyone he'd invited to the opening had accepted; tomorrow promised to be a day to warm a gallery owner's heart.

Late that night, as they lay together in their room, Rory tried one last, plaintive time.

"Would you please drop the other shoe, milady?"

Moving even closer to his side, she murmured sleepily, "Can't stand the heat, hero?"

"The suspense."

"Mmmm. It's good for your character, I'm sure."

"Witch."

When they arrived at the gallery the next afternoon, it was teeming with chattering people. David immediately met them, beaming, offering glasses of champagne and introductions. Rory enjoyed Banner's bemusement as people sincerely praised her work, and he stepped away from her to watch.

It was quite some time later that he became aware of someone staring at him, and turned his head to see a young lady who was a total stranger to him. As his eyes met hers, puzzled, she suddenly giggled and turned rather hastily away. Increasingly bewildered, he realized then that there was quite a bit of smothered laughter directed toward him. Uneasily aware that the shoe had somehow dropped without his noticing, Rory racked his brain, trying to figure out where it had landed.

Jake, who had wandered off to look over the paintings, suddenly materialized beside him. And the older man looked as if he were about to burst out laughing. "My boy," he said unsteadily, "I sincerely hope and trust you have a strong ego."

Rory looked at him with foreboding. "Will you please tell me what she's done?" he requested carefully.

Even more unsteadily, Jake said, "I think—she's made damned sure the punishment—fit the crime. You sprang the show on her, so . . . so she's springing something on you—at the show."

Taking a deep breath, Rory said, "Where is it?"

Jake gestured helplessly. "Just around the corner there."

Warily, Rory made his way around the corner indicated, studiously avoiding the smiling people staring at him. He rounded the corner, stopped . . . and his reaction—after the momentary impulse hurriedly to find himself a quiet, dark corner—was sheer rueful amusement.

Banner had gotten even. Oh, *how* she had gotten even.

The painting—tagged not for sale—was remarkably well done, especially considering the few days she'd had to work on it and the fact that she'd painted entirely from memory. He now knew why she'd "moved" her equipment and materials, and why she had disappeared so frequently these last days.

And he knew why laughing eyes kept following him.

Morning sunlight bathed the veranda in the foreground and the rose garden in the background. And on the veranda stood an obviously furious blond man with a brilliant green bedsheet wrapped togalike around him. His hands were clutching slipping linen, and both his tousled hair and morning stubble indicated a rude awakening of some kind. And if Rory had dared to ignore the similarity between this man and himself, Banner had carefully provided a positive identification by detailing the fire-opal signet ring he always wore on his right hand.

He realized he was grinning, and heard the muffled sounds of chuckles trying to escape. Roll with the punches, Jake'd advised? Hell, the little witch had punched below his belt! But he couldn't get mad, for some reason. He just made an emphasized, capitalized, underlined note to himself never again to get *her* mad.

With an effort, he managed to get his face straightened out and sober. Shoring up the mental shields around his bruised ego, he turned and stoically ran the gauntlet of those amused faces again, until he was standing before Banner.

She was alone for the first time since they'd come in, sipping a glass of champagne and watching his approach with a meditative air. When he stood staring down at her, she said only, "Want your ring back?" in a very calm voice.

"Milady," he said carefully, "I don't think I've ever had vengeance wreaked on me quite so thoroughly before now."

"Thank you," she responded politely.

"My cgo's in shreds."

"I thought it might be."

"My pride is in my shoes."

"These Clairmont women," she mourned sympathetically.

"I don't think I've ever been so damned embarrassed in front of total strangers."

"Poor man."

"And Jake will never again be able to look at me with a straight face."

She lifted a gently inquiring eyebrow and waited.

"If I were a reasonably sane, self-preserving male," he said musingly, "I would run like hell from a woman who not only has a talent for devious revenge, but also knows damned well I'm not going to run anywhere at all."

"Now, how could I know that?" she asked innocently. "I did ask if you wanted your ring back."

"You're a witch."

"So you've said."

"I should walk out that door right now."

"A sane man would," she agreed seriously.

"Will you swear never to do this to me again?"

"I'll never do this particular thing to you again," she said promptly.

"Because you never repeat yourself?"

"Uh-huh."

"But if I make you mad, you'll still get even somehow?"

"What can I say?"

"I should definitely walk out that door."

"Oh, definitely."

"Revenge is childish, you know."

"Certainly."

"Still... when I waltz with a Rebel, I guess I should expect to get my toes stepped on from time to time."

"Only when you step on mine first."

"I guess I'd better be careful from now on, huh?"

"That might be best."

"Safer, anyway."

"Uh-huh. Want your ring back?"

"Are you kidding?" He reached out to take her glass, setting it on a handy table, then pulled her into his arms with a fine disregard for all the people milling around. "I know a good thing when I latch on to one."

Banner smiled slowly, her own arms sliding

around his waist. "Now I can say it," she murmured.

"Say what?"

"Thank you for saving my Tara, darling."

"I didn't save it." He nodded around at the paintings surrounding them, most with "sold" stickers next to them. "You saved it."

"I know who saved it," she said huskily, and stood on tiptoes to kiss him.

At Rory's request, Banner wore an antebellum-style gown for their wedding, in the rose garden of Jasmine Hall. Jake gave her away and Rory's mother, Laura, who had been a guest at the Hall for the past several weeks, was her matron of honor. And the entire neighborhood, along with numerous acquaintances from Charleston, turned out.

Since the couple had decided to defer their honeymoon for a few days and planned to remain at the Hall, there was no great rush to change clothes for a bridal trip; everyone ended up making a party day of it.

Banner and Rory wandered together among the guests in the garden, she still in her ruffled gown and he in a tuxedo, and it wasn't until late in the afternoon that they found themselves alone together.

"Too late to back out now, Mrs. Stewart," he told her firmly, rubbing a possessive thumb across the wide band now accompanying her diamond.

"I could say the same for you," she reminded him. "You're the one who has to put up with my peculiar Clairmont temper from now on."

"If you *know* it's peculiar, why can't you do something about it?" he asked, curious.

"Like become rational?"

"It's just a thought, you understand."

"Well, unfortunately for you, when I get mad I follow my instincts."

"And they say get even?"

"You should know."

"Don't remind me." He sighed. "I can only be

thankful that the damned painting isn't hanging in the main hall."

"I like it in our bedroom."

"And I know why. You just want to be sure I never forget how a Clairmont woman gets even."

"Think of the embarrassment it'll save you in the future."

He grinned suddenly. "Well, I'm delighted with the way things turned out, milady, but weren't you taking quite a chance, with that painting? Were you so certain I wouldn't be furious enough to leave you?"

"I was certain." She smiled just a little.

"How? Because you were sure I loved you? Because you understand me so well?" He was honestly curious.

She nodded. "Yes. And a...couple of other things."

"What things?" Rory pulled her down beside him on a garden bench.

"For one..." She rubbed her nose in that rueful little way that fascinated him oddly. "Rory, do you remember that first day?"

"Here at the Hall? Of course."

"When we were together in the upstairs hallway, and again when we waltzed together that night, you saw some Rebel soldiers and their ladies. Remember?"

"I remember. In the ballroom, they waltzed with us."

"Yes. Well... I caught a glimpse of them upstairs, but during the waltz..."

"What're you trying to tell me?" he asked—but knew.

"They were ghosts, Rory. In the ballroom, no one but you saw them."

He'd learned to accept the ghostly presences of Jasmine Hall, and this latest addition hardly surprised him. "All right. And so?"

"I looked up a few of the old legends and ghost stories in the Hall book that night. And according to legend, only those who'll live their lives at the Hall will see the soldiers and their brides. The legend also says that if they dance the midnight waltz with an engaged couple, they're expressing approval of the union."

"So since I saw the soldiers, you knew I'd live at the Hall?"

"I thought it was a good bet."

"You saw them, too, you said."

"Vaguely. Hazily. But you instantly assumed you were looking at guests, so you saw them clearly. Darling, I've known since that night that you'd live in the Hall; I just wasn't sure that I would."

"Is that why you led me such a merry chase, milady?"

"You know why. I was convinced I'd lose both you and my home no matter what happened. When we took that suicidal jump that night, I was shocked into realizing I had to trust you . . . because I loved you too much not to."

He lifted her hand briefly to his lips. "So a legend about ghostly soldiers made you pretty sure I wouldn't leave you?"

"Pretty sure."

"You said there were a couple of things?"

"Well, the other thing was my Clairmont blood."

"I'm going to hate myself for asking this, I know, but what did that have to do with it?"

Banner smiled. "Darling, the Clairmonts have been many things, but they've never been quitters. Once you—uh—caught me, I wasn't about to let you go."

"I'm not sure who caught whom."

"Is it important?" she murmured.

"No." He smiled slowly. "It isn't important at all, milady."

Banner was just about to go into his arms when she stiffened suddenly, gazing past his shoulder. "Rory—look," she whispered.

Rory turned his head, his eyes immediately finding the tall blond man dressed in antebellum clothing who was standing several yards away from them. He was in the late-afternoon shadows of tall shrubbery, but remarkably distinct for all of that.

As they watched, still and silent, the blond gent made a slight gesture toward them, as a man would gesture politely for another to take his place with a dance partner. Then he bowed slightly, gracefully, and stepped back, vanishing into the dark shrubbery.

"I didn't believe it," Banner said blankly.

"What—that I've been seeing him all this time?" Rory asked, turning back to her. Then he realized that she had obviously seen him this time.

"No, I believed that." She gazed up at her husband. "But it was something else I read that first night."

"About the blond man?"

"Yes. According to legend, the Clairmont daughters never see their guardian—except once: when he renounces his guardianship of them in favor of their husbands."

Rory got to his feet and pulled her gently up. "I think," he said, smiling, "that the final mark of favor has been granted to our marriage, milady."

"A good omen."

"If we needed it. But I don't think we do. I think that you and I, wife, will never need more luck than we can make for ourselves. And I think we're going to have a great many happy years together." He grinned suddenly. "I also think we'd better provide another generation of Clairmont daughters for that blond gent to guard."

"You do, do you?" she murmured, gazing up at him.

"Certainly. We wouldn't want him to get bored, after all."

"I think... that's an awfully good idea, love. But maybe I'd better warn you about the Clairmonts."

"Oh, God," he said, sending a plaintive glance upward. "What now?"

Banner's smile was trying hard to hide. "Well, we tend to go to extremes, you see. Either we'll have a very small new generation—or a very large one. And it's about time for a large generation...."

EPILOGUE

"I SHOULD BE there," Rory said, pacing violently.

"You'd just be in the way."

"That's a hell of a thing to say to me!"

"But true. You've been a basket case for months, as it is."

"Your imagination. And hers."

"Hardly, my boy. How many breakfasts have you skipped?"

"I picked up a bug, that's all."

"Of course you did. But it only affected you in the mornings."

"That's nonsense."

"Have a drink."

"No. My child won't smell liquor on my breath when we meet."

"Shawn did," Jake reminded, amused, from the depths of his comfortable chair as he watched his grandson-in-law pacing the library.

Rory glared at him, still pacing. "Only because you put a drink in my hand and I didn't know what I was doing," he accused.

Jake sighed. "If I'd had any sense, I would have done the same thing hours ago." He was quiet for a moment, then said softly, "Did you know that Shawn can see Sarah?"

His grim expression softening, Rory halted by the fireplace and gazed down into the low flames. "I know. The pretty lady who smells so good. Do I explain to a two-year-old that she's his grandmother—and a ghost?"

"What does Banner say about it?"

"That he understands without really knowing."

"She's probably right. She understood at that age."

Rory's head lifted, his face turning toward the stairs and the silence. "Dammit," he swore softly, his expression tightening again. "I wish they'd tell us something!"

"She'll be fine, Rory."

"I should be with her!" He sighed roughly. "She seems to understand that, too, but I feel—"

"You can't stand seeing her in pain," Jake said quietly. "She knows that, Rory."

The younger man's haunted gaze met the steady older eyes. "It took so long with Shawn," he said tautly. "And she's so tiny. We both love kids, but—God, this scares the hell out of me!"

"Raynor would've put her in the hospital if he'd expected trouble," Jake pointed out soothingly. "He's a damn fine doctor."

"I know, I know. And Susan's the same nurse who helped with Shawn. I *know* all that, Jake— but it doesn't help."

The sound of footsteps on the stairs made

them both freeze, and they were still in a wax-works position when the cheerful, dark-haired and bright-eyed Dr. Raynor entered the room, rubbing his hands together briskly.

"I could use a drink," he said firmly.

"Matt?" Rory managed unsteadily, still frozen.

Raynor accepted a glass from Jake and took a healthy swallow. "That little lady fooled me this time," he said, shaking his head ruefully. "Since she carried so small with Shawn and so large with this one, I could have sworn it was twins."

"Matt!" Rory groaned.

The doctor smiled at him. "Banner's fine, Rory. She breezed right through this time."

A large part of the tension drained from Rory's face, but he continued to gaze at the doctor in mute inquiry.

"You get to pass out cigars with pink bands this time," Raynor told him cheerfully.

"A girl?"

Raynor was abruptly solemn, clearly relishing his role of announcer. "Oh, yes, indeed. Like I said—Banner fooled me. You've got yourself... three brand-new daughters, Rory."

"Triplets?" Rory was sure he said the word, but heard no sound emerge from his own mouth. Jake handed him a glass, and he found himself swallowing fiery liquid. He tried again. "Can I—can I go up and see them?" he croaked. He barely waited for the doctor's smiling nod before he headed for the stairs.

Susan was coming out of the bedroom just as he reached it, and she was laughing softly. "Banner's amazing," she told him dryly. "I've never seen a woman have even *one* baby and still find the energy to sit up. She's in there looking through a dictionary of names. Amazing." Shaking her head, the nurse went on down the hall.

Rory crept into the bedroom, wary of disturbing three newborns. And found his wife, as Susan had said, sitting up in the bed and frowning down at the heavy book across her knees. She looked not one bit the worse for the past hours; in fact, she seemed wide awake and rested. And when she looked up, her green eyes were bright.

"I know we wanted a girl, Rory," she said with a comical look of amazement on her face, "but I think we overdid it a bit."

He sat on the edge of the bed and put his arms around her, kissing her smiling lips very tenderly. "I love you."

"I love you too." She was still smiling. "Even if you have been drinking."

"Jake caught me with my guard down again," he explained.

"That was your excuse the last time."

"I swear. Matt said three girls and Jake put a glass in my hand."

"Well, I'll forgive you. *If* you can help me come up with three names. And a mixed bag this time—blond, brunette, and redhead."

He blinked, then shook his head. "I can't think at the moment."

"I can't imagine why," she said gravely. "Unless it's because you're exhausted. Go take a look at the babies, darling, then come to bed."

"With you?" he said longingly.

"I got permission to hold you," she said, still grave. "Matt was quite firm about saying we could not start another baby for several weeks."

Laughing a little unsteadily, Rory got to his feet. "The mess you've gotten me into," he accused, then headed for the connecting nursery.

As he stepped into the dimly-lighted room, Rory noted that the efficent nurse had utilized both the crib and bassinet, along with the old wooden cradle that had been Jake's, in order to accommodate all three infants. And he wasn't really surprised to see the hazy—though clearer than he'd ever seen it—form of the blond gentleman bending to get a look at the babies. Rory stood silently and watched until, apparently satisfied, the gent moved toward the hall door.

Softly, Rory said, "Three more Clairmont daughters for you to guard, my friend. For us both to guard."

He could have sworn the gent smiled at him.

Smiling himself, Rory went to greet his daughters.

ABOUT THE AUTHOR

KAY HOOPER is the award-winning author of *Blood Sin*, *Blood Dreams*, *Sleeping with Fear*, *Hunting Fear*, *Chill of Fear*, *Touching Evil*, *Whisper of Evil*, *Sense of Evil*, *Once a Thief*, *Always a Thief*, the Shadows trilogy, and other novels. She lives in North Carolina, where she is at work on her next book.

Read on for a special preview of
the second thrilling novel in
Kay Hooper's Blood trilogy . . .

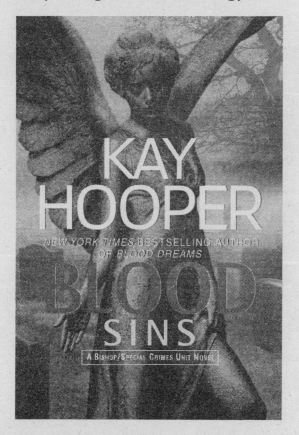

Now on sale from Bantam

BLOOD SINS

On sale now

Sarah kept to what little shadows the winter-bare trees provided as she worked her way through the forest that separated the compound from the road. The full moon made this night an uneasy one for stealth, but she hadn't been given much choice in the matter. Waiting even another day was potentially far more dangerous than acting, so—

She sensed more than heard a sound, and froze, her arms tightening around the sleeping child.

"It's just me." Bailey appeared to step literally out of the darkness not ten feet away.

"Are you early or am I late?" Sarah kept her voice as low as the other woman's had been.

"Six of one." Bailey shrugged and crossed the space between them. "Is she out?"

Nodding, Sarah relinquished the little girl, who was warmly dressed to protect her against the January chill. "She should sleep another couple of hours at least. Long enough."

"And you're sure about her? Because we can't keep doing this. It wasn't part of the plan, and it's too dangerous. Sooner or later, he's going to figure it out."

"That's what I'm trying to prevent. Or at least delay."

"It's not your job, Sarah. Not the reason you're here."

"Isn't it? He's getting better at choosing latents. Better at finding them and convincing them to join him. Better than we've been." Sarah was aware of a niggling unease that was growing rather than diminishing. "Speaking of, are we covered?"

"Of course. My shield's enclosing all three of us."

"What about more conventional protection?"

"Galen's got my back. As usual. But once we leave, you're on your own again."

"I'm not worried about me."

"Sarah—"

"She could be the one, Bailey."

"She's six years old."

"All the more reason. Without the defenses we can teach her, she's vulnerable as hell, especially to someone bent on using her as a weapon."

Bailey shifted the slight weight of the child and sighed. "Look, are you sure you haven't been . . . influenced . . . by what this guy is preaching? All that prophecy stuff?"

"We believe in prophecy stuff," Sarah reminded her.

"Not the kind he preaches."

Sarah shook her head. "Don't worry, I'm not a convert. It's all I can do to keep up the facade of a loyal member of the flock."

"Many more defections and kids disappearing, and that's going to get a lot harder."

"Harder than this?" Sarah reached out a hand and lightly touched the long blond hair hanging down the child's back. "Her mother is gone. And her father vanished day before yesterday."

Bailey's mouth tightened. "You didn't include that in the report."

"I wasn't sure until today. But he's gone. I think he was beginning to ask too many questions. He didn't believe his wife would have just run away, not without their daughter."

"He was right about that."

Sarah had been expecting it, but the news was still an unwelcome shock. "She was found?"

"A few miles downriver. And she'd been in the water awhile, probably since the night she disappeared. No way to determine cause of death."

Bailey didn't have to explain that further.

"Are the police going to come around asking questions?" Sarah asked.

"They have to. Ellen Hodges was known to be a member of the Church, and the last time she was seen it was in the company of other Church members. Her parents know that, and they're more than willing to point the police in this direction. So if the good Reverend Samuel can't produce Ellen's husband *or* her child, he's going to have a lot of explaining to do."

Sarah managed a hollow laugh, even as the sense of unease she felt grew stronger. "You're assuming the cops who come here won't be Church members or paid-off *friends* of the Church."

"Shit. Are you sure?"

"From something I overheard, I'm convinced enough that I say it wouldn't be a good idea to take any local law enforcement into our confidence. Not unless somebody on our side can read them very, very well."

"Good enough for me. But Bishop is not going to be happy about it."

"I doubt he'll be surprised. We knew it was a possibility."

"Makes the job harder. Or at least a hell of a lot more tricky." Bailey shifted the child's weight again. "I need to get the kid out of here."

"Wendy. Her name's Wendy."

"Yes. I know. Don't worry, we'll take care of her. She has family who love her and will want her."

"She also has an ability she's barely aware of." Sarah reached out once more to gently touch the child's hair, then stepped back. "Protect her. Protect her gift."